The Chocolate Spy

The Crime Solving Cousins Mystery Series

The Feather Chase

The Treasure Key

The Chocolate Spy

The Chocolate Spy

A Crime-Solving Cousins Mystery

Shannon L. Brown

Sienna Bay Press

Sienna Bay Press
PO Box 158582
Nashville, TN 37215

www.shannonlbrown.com

The Chocolate Spy/Shannon L. Brown—1st ed.

ISBN: 978-1-945527-12-8

Library of Congress Control Number: 2017917425

To all of the amazing readers
of the Crime-Solving Cousins Mysteries,
thank you for being part of
Sophie and Jessica's adventures!

1

Something's Up

Jessica Ballow put her sunglasses on and lay down on her towel on Pine Lake's sandy beach.

Her cousin, Sophie Sandoval, sat on a beach towel next to her. "So what should we do now?"

Jessica let out a big sigh. "This is pretty good. My heart isn't racing every fifteen minutes now that we've wrapped up our last mystery. My summer in small-town Pine Hill has been much more exciting than I expected, even more exciting than back home in the big city of London, England."

"Even I'm not quite ready to search for a new mystery. But if one found me, I guess I'd be open."

Jessica laughed. "You are *always* ready for a mystery."

Sophie pointed into the distance. "Hey, there's Tony over on Main Street, handing something out to people."

Jessica sat up and slid her sunglasses down her nose. "He's coming this direction. Is my hair okay?"

She smoothed her blonde hair, then tucked it behind her ears.

Sophie looked her over. "Great, as usual."

They watched Tony Donadio make his way across the street and toward them on the sand. Tony's parents owned Donadio's Deli, where Jessica and Sophie often ate. He was also more than a little bit cute, went to the same church Sophie and Jessica attended, and was super smart like her.

When he reached the girls, he handed a sheet of paper down to Sophie. Jessica leaned over to peer at it. On it was printed: *Have a sweet summer. Learn how to make chocolates. Classes at Sweet Bites Chocolates now open.*

"Hmm," said Sophie. "Are you interested, Jessica? It's at a chocolate factory not far from here."

Jessica turned toward Sophie. "It doesn't involve a mystery. And it's chocolate? Do you even need to ask?"

Sophie laughed, and Tony grinned.

Tony said, "I knew you'd ordered hot fudge sundaes a couple of times over at the deli, but I didn't realize you had a thing for chocolate."

"Oh yeah. The resort makes those awesome triple chocolate shakes, and there are the sundaes you've made for me at Donadio's Deli. How could I have missed a chocolate factory while I've been visiting here?"

"Not only is it a factory, but my uncle owns it. I'm handing these out for him." Tony held up the stack of papers.

"Your uncle?" Sophie asked. "My class went to see a chocolate factory a couple of years ago, but I thought it was owned by a family named the Wongs."

"My Uncle Sal bought it from them earlier this year. He lived all over the world while he was in the Army and wanted to settle down someplace when he got out."

"Your uncle learned to make candy in the military?" Sophie asked.

Tony laughed. "No. He repaired helicopters in the army. Uncle Sal liked it here when he visited my family, the business was for sale, and he loves chocolate, so he was pretty excited to buy it. The good news is that my family gets samples every once in a while."

Jessica looked at the flyer again. "I wonder if we'll get samples if we take this class."

Tony shrugged. "Probably."

Sophie sighed. "Jessica has been trying to get me to like chocolate. It's *okay*. But I don't want to run toward it every time I see some."

Jessica said, "And I do. For cousins, we're very different."

"That's true!" Tony and Sophie said together.

The three of them laughed.

"Sophie, let's go see your mom and ask if we can take this class."

"I think Mom will be very happy to know where we are while the classes are going on—and that we aren't in the middle of a mystery."

"You two managed to get into the middle of some danger with *The Feather Chase* and *The Treasure Key*," Tony said.

"Not just the two of us, Tony. You were right in the middle of it too. *Three* twelve-year-olds solved the mysteries."

Tony shrugged. "We have had some exciting times this summer. I hope you'll let me know if you find another mystery."

Jessica shuddered. "Whew. I hope that doesn't happen."

Sophie nudged Jessica with her elbow. "You know you had fun. But could we find another mystery this soon? Even I wonder about that."

A loud sound came from over the hills in the direction of Cutoff Trail. Sophie, Jessica, and Tony all turned toward it. A helicopter flew toward heir direction, barely above the many tall pine trees that gave this town its name. Sand blew around them as it passed overhead.

Jessica covered her eyes with her hands, only pulling them away when the sound faded. The aircraft now hovered in the sky on the opposite side of town, then dropped below the trees and buildings.

Sophie stood and brushed herself off. "Wow! A helicopter! I think it landed near the resort."

Jessica combed her hair with her fingers. "What's so unusual about a helicopter? I see lots of them."

"Not in Pine Hill. I only remember seeing a couple. And it turned out later that someone was very sick, and the helicopter had come to take them to the hospital. Oh no! I hope everyone there is okay."

Sophie grabbed her towel and shook it out. Jessica stood and did the same. They both rolled their towels up as they started walking toward the helicopter's landing spot at the top of a nearby hill with Tony at their side.

When they crested the hill and could see the front of the fancy resort hotel, they also saw people they knew crowded around in front of it. Businesses around town must have closed with the sound of the helicopter so their owners and workers could rush to see what had happened.

Tony said, "There's a landing pad on top of the resort. The construction crew came into our deli and bought lunch a few times while they were building it a few months ago. I didn't think anyone would ever use it."

One person was pointing at the roof, so Jessica guessed it was as Tony had suggested: the aircraft had landed on the roof of the resort. Mrs. Bowman, the owner of Bananas Bakery, was among the onlookers, and they all knew her, so they hurried over there.

When they reached her, the older woman glanced briefly at the trio, then returned her gaze to the roof. Before they could even ask what happened, Mrs. Bowman said, "Did you see it? A helicopter just landed up there. Tony's dad went inside to check and make sure someone isn't sick. If they are, we could get Doc Adams to come over here to help. The people working at the resort may not know about him."

Mr. Donadio came out of the resort with a smile on his face and said to the small crowd, "Everything's fine. We can all leave. They had a guest arrive in a helicopter. I guess that can happen now that they have the helipad on the roof, so we don't need to worry every time we hear the flapping sound of a helicopter."

Someone said, "Good!" and others agreed.

"Mrs. Bowman and I should mention that you can have a wonderful lunch at Donadio's Deli and follow it up with a delicious baked good, such as a muffin or a piece of cheesecake, over at Bananas Bakery."

"Please do," added Mrs. Bowman.

Smiles on faces told Jessica that some of the people in the crowd might do that.

Jessica watched everyone walk away, including Tony, who headed back with his parents to the deli. "Sophie, do you think he minds working in the summer?"

"No. I asked him once. He likes helping out his family, and he still gets to do other things, like when he works with us." Sophie looked in the direction of the deli. "It's downtown, so it's also close to a lot of things."

"I'm not sure I'd be that nice," Jessica said.

Just then, a man came out of the resort and

hurried away. He glanced over his shoulder as he went around the corner of the building and toward the center of Pine Hill. The man wore a suit and tie and sunglasses, and he reminded her very much of Agent Dallas, the FBI agent they'd met while working on a mystery.

"Sophie? Did you see that man go around the side of the building?"

Sophie turned back. "What? Where?"

Jessica pointed.

"Did he seem suspicious or mysterious?" Sophie asked with too much excitement in her voice, more than Jessica wanted to hear. She'd had enough of mysteries forever.

Jessica shrugged, trying to act casual so that Sophie wouldn't become too interested and try to follow him. "He was a man in a suit. I know you've said before that there aren't very many of those in town."

"It's probably just another man here to do business."

Jessica didn't say anything, but she wondered about that. Could the helicopter have brought a new mystery to Pine Hill?

2

Can You Keep a Secret?

After leaving the resort, Sophie and Jessica hurried over to Great Finds, the antique shop owned by Sophie's mother. When they got there, they pushed open the glass door, and a bell announced their arrival. Sophie called out, "Mom, it's just us."

April Sandoval stepped into the doorway of her back room, drying her hands on a towel. "I was washing up some new teacups and vases."

"We went to see who was in the helicopter."

"Helicopter?" Mrs. Sandoval tossed the towel off to the side. "I guess I didn't hear it over the running water. Who's in trouble?"

"No one," Sophie answered. "It's okay, Mom. I didn't know that the resort had a helipad now, and it was just someone coming to stay there."

"I knew they'd built it, but I didn't think anybody would ever use it."

Jessica smiled. "That's what Tony said."

Sophie handed her mom the class announcement

that Tony had given them, and she read it. Looking up at the two of them, she asked, "Do you want to go to this?"

"Sure." Sophie shrugged.

Jessica nodded. "It's chocolate."

"Well, it sounds like a good way for me to know where you are several mornings in the next week." She glanced at the flyer. "I wonder why the classes skip days in between. Anyway, you'll be there bright and early in the morning."

"Morning? I didn't notice the time, Mom." Sophie leaned over to read the paper again.

"You'll need to leave the house before me. If you come to Great Finds after class, you can help me. When you do, I'll treat you to lunch at the deli. Jessica should like that."

Jessica smiled at the thought of seeing Tony at lunchtimes.

"But Mom—"

Mrs. Sandoval gave Sophie a look that told her she wouldn't win this one.

"Okay, Mom. The morning class."

Jessica wasn't too happy about the time either. Morning definitely wasn't her favorite part of the day.

"Unless you don't want to go, Jessica."

"I love chocolate, so I guess I'm willing to get up early."

With Sophie and Jessica looking over her shoulder, Mrs. Sandoval picked up the phone and dialed the number on the paper. "Sophie," she said as she waited for someone to answer her call, "can you take the trash outside to the Dumpster, please? There's some here and more in the back room."

"Sure, Mom," Sophie answered. She picked up the trash can, which was full to the brim, and carried it out the back door. "Be right back," she said to Jessica.

As Jessica heard her aunt tell the person why she'd called, she glanced toward the window and saw Sheriff Valeska walk by the front of the shop. If anyone knew whether or not the FBI was back in town, the sheriff certainly would.

"I'm going to run out and see if the sheriff knows who was in the helicopter, okay?" Her aunt gave a nod of agreement, so Jessica hurried outside. Anywhere else, she might have used her cell phone to ask her question, but with the hills surrounding Pine Hill, you never knew if a cell phone would work or not.

The sheriff had stopped to talk to a man about half a block away. Jessica waited until the man walked off before she moved closer.

When Jessica had met Sheriff Valeska the first time, she'd expected a sheriff to be hard-as-nails, like the sheriffs and police officers she'd seen on TV and in the movies. She'd been surprised to find a woman sheriff, and Sheriff Valeska did a great job. While she might not always appreciate Sophie's tips about possible mysteries, because Sophie often saw mysteries when there weren't any, she'd been very kind when they had found a real one. She'd also let them do some things that Jessica wasn't sure every sheriff would allow kids to do.

When the sheriff started in the opposite direction, Jessica called out, "Sheriff! Sheriff!"

Sheriff Valeska turned back and paused to allow Jessica to catch up with her.

"What can I help you with?"

Jessica glanced around to make sure no one could overhear them. "I saw a man who might be an FBI agent. He was dressed like one. Are the FBI back in Pine Hill?"

Sheriff Valeska stood there silently for a moment, then said, "Even if I knew, Jessica, I couldn't tell you."

Jessica's shoulders dropped. "Is there another mystery?"

Sheriff Valeska paused again before saying, "You, Sophie, and Tony have worked together on other mysteries. Tony's uncle owns the chocolate factory, you know."

Jessica nodded. "Sophie and I are going to take a chocolate-making class there starting tomorrow." She hoped the word *mysteries* and the chocolate factory didn't connect in any way.

Now it was Sheriff Valeska who turned to look around, and Jessica guessed she was also making sure no one could hear what she was about to say. Jessica hoped it was *good* news.

"I can't tell you very much . . ." The sheriff seemed to be gathering her thoughts and deciding how to say her next words. Finally, she said, "I'd like to ask you to keep your eyes open when you're at the chocolate factory."

"Keep my eyes open? For what?"

"Anything that seems not quite right."

This was starting to feel more like something Sophie would like to be involved in. "What does 'not quite right' mean?" When the sheriff didn't answer, Jessica thought about what could be wrong in a chocolate factory. "A thief?"

Sheriff Valeska shifted her hat farther back on her head. "Someone may not be who they say they are."

"A spy?"

"I can't tell you any more. Now, I have to ask three things of you. One, don't tell anyone else. Two, anyone else means Sophie."

Oh no. She couldn't tell mystery-loving Sophie about a possible mystery in her town?

"We don't know much yet," the sheriff explained. "And Sophie has a way of getting herself in the middle of things."

Sophie did have a way of finding danger. "I won't tell her right now. To protect her."

The sheriff nodded. "The third thing is that if you discover something, don't talk to anyone about it but me. Don't trust anyone else with this. Do you understand?"

Panic surged through Jessica. Not only might there be another mystery in Pine Hill, but she alone could end up right at the center of it. She gulped. "I understand, Sheriff. I won't let you down."

They said good-bye to each other, and Jessica went back to Great Finds where she found her aunt still on the phone, finishing up their reservations for the class. The class still sounded good, but Jessica now wondered what else she was signing up for.

Sophie returned from trash duty. As she reached them, her mother was setting the phone down.

Mrs. Sandoval said, "Class begins tomorrow. The woman on the phone, Erma Clayton, explained that they're teaching the classes around the schedule for their orders. That's why you'll be there Wednesday, Saturday, Monday, and Tuesday instead of four days in a row."

"That's plenty of chocolate for me," Sophie said.

"One important rule is that people in the factory aren't allowed to wear perfume because the scent can get into the chocolate just by being near it and change the taste. The class sounds like fun. Maybe you can bring some chocolate home for us."

Sophie stared suspiciously at her mother. "Who is this person in front of me? We don't have dessert in our house very often, so what you're saying doesn't make sense. Are you telling me that you like chocolate, Mom?"

Her mom smiled. "I may not believe we should have dessert every day, but that doesn't mean I don't like it. If we had some chocolate treats for a week, our family—including Jessica, of course—could take a little break from my no-sugar plan, and I would join you."

Sophie sat on the stool behind the cash register. "I'm twelve years old, and I just learned Mom's shocking secret."

Jessica grinned. "My mother loves chocolate, so I was surprised yours didn't. Now I understand. She loves it too." She glanced over at her aunt, who nodded. "But she doesn't eat it all the time."

Mrs. Sandoval nodded again.

The bell on the door rang as Sheriff Valeska came into the shop. Jessica picked up a feather duster and swept it over the shelves—her least favorite thing to do at Great Finds—but this way she'd have her back to everyone, so the expression on her face couldn't reveal her secret with the sheriff.

Mrs. Sandoval asked, "Mandy, have you caught the guy yet?"

Sophie turned toward her mom. "What guy, Mom? What happened?"

"I'm surprised you haven't heard, Sophie. Someone stole a car that was parked right here on Main Street."

Jessica turned to them with her feather duster in midair. "In Pine Hill?"

The sheriff rubbed her hand over her face. "I wish they hadn't done it. I'm visiting each of the shops on Main Street to make sure no one saw the theft, that nothing suspicious had happened this morning."

"Everything is perfectly normal here, Mandy," Mrs. Sandoval said.

"Well, I set up a checkpoint on the highway

leading out of town. We're stopping every car. I don't like doing that because I don't want this to seem like an unfriendly town, but I have to find the stolen car."

More crimes and criminals? If Jessica were alone with the sheriff, she would ask if this could be connected to what she'd asked her to do.

"Right, Jessica?" Sophie said.

Jessica almost jumped out of her skin when she heard her name. She turned around.

Sophie, Aunt April, and Sheriff Valeska all stared at her.

What had they been saying? With Sophie, she never knew. "Um. Right?"

"You'll catch him, Sheriff," Sophie said.

"Unless they escaped with the car before we realized they'd stolen it. But I hope we do, Sophie."

The sheriff left.

Jessica brought the subject back to chocolate to distract her aunt and cousin in case they'd noticed she'd acted strangely around the sheriff. "Aunt April, we'll do our best to bring you samples every day."

Mrs. Sandoval said, "I like that idea. When you're there, you may notice that Sweet Bites Chocolates is in an unusual building. Long before I was born, it was the boathouse for a big country club down at the water's edge. A boathouse sits over the water, and boats are kept in it."

"That sounds like a garage, Aunt April. Are there still boats there?"

"They're long gone. They used to be in the water underneath today's factory. They had parties and weddings where the factory is. The larger, even more elegant building next door burned down." She turned to Sophie. "Before they made chocolate in the boathouse and before you were born, it was a restaurant, and your father and I would go to eat dinner and watch the sun set over the water."

Mrs. Sandoval laughed. "I went there once to talk to a friend who worked in the restaurant. Her office was down a hallway that turned into another hallway and turned a corner and went around that corner and down steps and up steps. It was crazy. You'll have to let me know if they've opened it all up, or if there are still all kinds of odd places there."

It sounded exactly like the type of place where they'd find a mystery. Jessica hoped that wouldn't happen, that she wouldn't learn *anything* interesting to tell the sheriff.

3

A Sweet Class

Sophie sat up in bed and rubbed her eyes, trying to wake up. Moving as quietly as she could, she stepped onto the floor and tiptoed over to the bathroom so she could take a shower. Not long after Jessica had come to stay with her for the summer, Sophie had learned her cousin wasn't good at waking up. When Sophie had finished showering, she put on her robe, then slowly opened the bathroom door.

Jessica was sitting up. Without saying a word, she got out of bed and trudged by Sophie into the bathroom. Sophie stepped aside, the door closed behind her, and she heard the water turn on.

As Jessica showered, Sophie got dressed and dried her hair before pulling it back into a ponytail. A short time later, the bathroom door opened and her cousin came out, rubbing her hair with a towel. "My shower helped. I think I'm ready to face the day."

Sophie sat on the end of her bed. "This might be the earliest we've gotten up this summer. It almost—*almost*—makes getting up for school look good."

"This morning was a little easier than school. It involves chocolate." Jessica did a little happy dance, then began drying her hair, which Sophie knew would be followed by her putting on her makeup.

After what seemed like forever, Sophie groaned and flopped backward on the bed. "We're *just* taking a class, Jessica."

Jessica stepped back and checked her reflection in the mirror, then added earrings and a bracelet. "Almost ready. Notice that I'm wearing chocolate brown shorts to celebrate our first day making my favorite treat." She turned to face Sophie. "Let's go."

Sophie rolled off the bed. "I wish you could get ready as quickly as I do." She gestured toward her hair, then to her faded jeans and white T-shirt.

"I've stopped using a lot of my makeup since I came to Pine Hill, but I do like to have it just right."

They went through the living room and into the kitchen to get a bite to eat. Sophie made toast for both of them while Jessica poured juice. When they were seated at the small kitchen table, Sophie said, "I wish we had a mystery. Well, at least part of me wishes we had a mystery."

Jessica coughed and reached for her juice.

"Are you okay?"

After taking another sip of juice, she said, "Fine."

"Aren't you going to say how happy you are that we *don't* have a mystery to work on?"

"Mysteries are interesting when you're in the middle of them, and always seem to end up dangerous, but are better than not doing anything." Jessica got to her feet and took her plate and glass over to the sink, rinsed them off, and put them in the dishwasher. "Today we get to make chocolates."

Sophie finished her toast and took her things to the dishwasher too. "It sounds fun to learn how to make chocolates, but I wish I wanted to eat what we've made."

"Did your mom say what she was going to have us do this afternoon at Great Finds?"

"She only said that she wanted us to come over and help. It could be something interesting, and it could be more dusting." Sophie grabbed her backpack and Jessica her purse, and they both went out the door, down the steps, and over to the trail that led through the woods.

The cousins followed the trail to Pine Hill, kept going through town and past the resort, then turned left toward the lake where the chocolate factory sat.

They soon approached a building painted a color that Sophie could best describe as "chocolate chip." A big sign with letters that looked like someone had taken bites out of them read, "Sweet Bites Chocolates." The building's large door was painted to look like a box of chocolate and the door handle like a chocolate bar.

Sophie pulled the door open and entered with Jessica right behind her. They stopped just inside the building. A desk to their right was empty, but she thought someone should be sitting there waiting to greet them.

A woman came around the corner in a hurry, panting. She stopped and gave them a big smile. "Hello, ladies. I'm Erma Clayton. I'm so sorry I wasn't here when you came in. I've taken three people back to the classroom area, and you must be two more for me." She sat down in front of her computer.

"Yes, ma'am," Jessica said. "I'm Jessica Ballow, and this is my cousin Sophie Sandoval."

The woman checked her computer screen, made a few clicks, then stood again, grabbing a couple of name tags as she did. She handed one to each of them. "We're happy to have you here for the class."

Sophie pinned her name tag to her shirt, and Jessica did the same.

Still smiling, Mrs. Clayton motioned for them to follow her. They all went down a hall, around a corner, and into a small room with some chairs set up and a screen on the wall. It could have been a classroom in a school anywhere. Sophie felt a bit of nervousness pass through her as she realized this might not be fun, there might not be treats to sample, and they might have to sit in a classroom for days learning how people made chocolates.

Her expression must have given away her thoughts. A man who looked like Tony's dad said, "Come in. Come in. Please find a seat." He watched the two of them walk over and sit down in chairs in the last of the four rows. A man and two women had arrived before them. "And don't worry. We'll only be in this classroom for a little while this morning. Most of the time, you're going to be out in the factory learning how to make chocolates."

Only one more person, an older man, arrived, then the man who'd greeted them walked to the front of the room and began. "I'm Salvatore Donadio. I've only lived in Pine Hill for half a year, but many of you, if not all of you, know my brother who owns Donadio's Deli." Everyone in the class nodded, then glanced at each other, smiling. Tony's dad had a great reputation in the town. Sophie and Jessica had wondered about him when they'd been working on their last mystery and had been glad when he'd checked out okay.

As Mr. Donadio walked across the room, he added, "The next class has twice this number of people signed up, probably because they had more time to plan for it. You're first so we'll learn how to do this together."

He dimmed the lights, returned to the front, and turned on a projector. Pictures of candy flashed onto the screen. Mr. Donadio then told his students the history of chocolate, how it was found in South America and that explorers brought it to Europe where it became very popular, and word about the delicious treat soon spread.

When he'd finished, he said, "Now I'm going to

take you on a tour of my beautiful chocolate factory. But first, do you have any questions?"

Sophie raised her hand, and he nodded in her direction.

"Do you only make chocolates here, or do you make other kinds of candy too?"

"Great question! We make more than thirty kinds of chocolate, different flavors, shapes, sizes—"

Sophie felt her heart sink at his words. This would be chocolate and nothing but that. She'd still try to have fun. Even if she didn't learn to love chocolate like Jessica did.

He gestured for the class to follow him, and one by one they went out the door, down the hall, and around another corner. Her mother had been right. This building had so many twists and turns that it was hard to know where she was.

Mr. Donadio stopped in front of a closed door, and his students crowded around him. "This is our storage area, where we keep some of our supplies." He unlocked the door, pushed it open, then stepped aside so they could see into the room.

A wide array of items sat on shelves piled with many different sizes of boxes for chocolates, jars, and cans of all sorts of things that Sophie couldn't even begin to guess what they were for in making candy. There were pens, pencils, and office paper. Mr. Donadio stepped into the room, picked up a box, and held it up. Sophie could see that it was marked "bubble gum."

"I had what I thought was a great idea," he said. "You can tell me if I was wrong, or if the people who have advised me are wrong." He reached into the box and pulled out a piece of what Sophie could tell was a kind of bubble gum she'd had before. Holding it up, he said, "I thought chocolate-covered bubble-gum would be a hit with our customers. What do you think?"

Sophie grimaced. Would that sound good to someone who loved chocolate?

A woman to her right said, "Sal, your company makes wonderful chocolates, but I think that sounds horrible."

Everyone seemed to agree.

Sophie thought his feelings would be hurt, but he just smiled and shrugged. "I'll come up with something new that people love. Chocolate-covered strawberries, those are all over the place, so I don't want to do more of them unless someone really wants them. I want to make something special, different, and quite wonderful."

He next took everyone toward the factory area. As they walked, he said to Sophie and Jessica, "You're friends with Tony, right?"

"Yes, sir," Sophie answered.

"That makes you like family to a Donadio, so please call me Uncle Sal, as Tony does."

"Uncle Sal" stopped at the entrance to the factory. "Here we make delicious chocolates. So that your hands are free, please leave your purses and other belongings behind Mrs. Clayton's desk while we're working."

When they'd done that, he led them into a room around the corner from the lobby. "This is where we keep our finished chocolates at the perfect temperature. You can each choose one."

A sigh went up from almost everyone there.

He put on gloves and picked up the piece of chocolate each person pointed to.

Jessica said, "I'll have anything dark chocolate." When she bit into it, she said, "Yum. Raspberry cream."

Sophie halfheartedly said, "I'll take whichever one you think is best, Uncle Sal." When she took a bite of the light chocolate piece, the orange flavor inside brought a smile to her face. Maybe this wouldn't be bad after all.

When they stepped out of the room, a worker called Uncle Sal over.

Walking away, he said, "Everyone, share your names. I'll be right back."

4

Oops!

One of the women in the chocolate-making class—Jessica didn't think she was quite as old as her mom—introduced herself as Emily Foster. "I'm here on vacation. Who could resist a chocolate class?"

A man about her grandfather's age said, "I'm Peter Pleckenpoll." Jessica wondered if she'd be able to remember that. He must have had that problem in the past because he added, "Please call me Mr. P."

Sophie grinned. "That's easy."

A young man with an older woman by his side gave his name as Dylan Hanley. "I'm working in Pine Hill for the summer as part of a college class. This is my mother, Beverly." Turning to the woman at his side, he added, "She's visiting."

"It's a pleasure to meet all of you," Mrs. Hanley said. "I'm enjoying my trip to Pine Hill. Are you from here?"

Jessica opened her mouth to answer, but she continued.

"I'm from Chicago. Dylan grew up there, didn't you, son?" Before he could reply, she said, "Summer isn't bad there, but winter can be cold."

Jessica glanced at Sophie, and her cousin shrugged. They both wanted to say something to be polite but were fairly certain the older woman wouldn't give them a chance. And, as expected, Mrs. Hanley picked up where her last sentence left off.

As she described her trip to Pine Hill in detail, Jessica listened but checked out the people in the class. None of them looked suspicious. Smart criminals would seem innocent though, wouldn't they?

At last Uncle Sal returned, interrupting the woman's story of her travel from the airport, and began his tour with some giant-sized pots to the side of the room. "This is where we keep the chocolate at a perfect melted temperature at all times. If chocolate isn't treated with care, it can get crystals in it and do other strange things, things that don't taste good and might not make a pretty piece of candy."

Jessica said, "We call candy 'sweets' in England."

Uncle Sal nodded. "Yes. My chocolates are sweets when they're sold there."

With a big smile on his face, he led them over to what he called the enrober, a long machine with a belt that carried pieces of candy filling into a shower of liquid chocolate. "We're making my favorite today, chocolate-covered marshmallows. We do them in both dark and milk chocolate, but today we're using milk chocolate."

Jessica would have rather had dark chocolate, but this should still be fun.

"Everyone will have a chance to put the marshmallows we make here on the belt at the beginning and to set the finished pieces on a tray at the end." Still smiling, he warned, "No sampling the finished chocolates."

At everyone's sad expression, he added, "But you can each have a piece of your choice later. Maybe two."

His students laughed.

"You and you,"—he pointed first to Sophie then to Jessica—"can be first on the beginning of the line. Emily and I will go to the end of the line. We only keep perfectly coated pieces of candy. I will teach her what to watch for, then have someone take my place so she can teach them."

Everyone put on plastic gloves. Then the four who were working the line took their positions.

"I hope we can move as fast as we're supposed to," Jessica said to Sophie.

A worker wheeled over a cart with trays of square pieces of marshmallow on it. The man set eight pieces in a row on the end of the belt where the bottoms were then coated with chocolate. They moved down the belt to be showered in a waterfall of chocolate, then slid out of sight into a long, enclosed section, what the man helping them said was the cooling tunnel where the chocolate hardened.

He stepped aside and watched as the two of them each put four pieces of marshmallow in a single row on the belt. Then seconds later, another row. With the third row, he nodded his approval and walked away.

They put row after row on the belt. When a cheer went up, Jessica glanced at the end of the machine. Emily and Uncle Sal were working, so she knew their first chocolates had made it to the end of the line. The rest of their class gathered there to see.

"Whew. This is harder than I realized," Sophie said. "We have to move more quickly, or they won't have as many chocolates made today as they should."

As she reached for more marshmallows, Jessica said, "Yes, it's intense." She lowered her arm, then realized she didn't feel the movement of her bracelet on her wrist. "Sophie, do you see my bracelet? I know I had it when we began."

When Sophie stepped back to check the area, Jessica said, "No, I don't want to mess up this job. Keep moving, but keep your eyes open too."

Jessica leaned back to check the floor as she set the next batch of marshmallows on the belt. Not there. She checked the tray they'd pulled the marshmallows from to see if her bracelet had dropped onto it. No.

A gasp made her turn in Sophie's direction. She

followed Sophie's gaze to the belt as it entered the cooling area. A chocolate-coated lump rested beside the covered marshmallows.

Jessica's heart sank to her toes. She whispered, "Uncle Sal will set it aside when it comes out."

Sophie snorted. "And tell everyone in his family." She grabbed four marshmallows and set them on the belt. When Jessica didn't do her half, Sophie grabbed another four and added them to her row.

Jessica felt her face grow hot. "Maybe he won't say anything."

"Are you kidding? Who could resist a story about a chocolate-covered bracelet?"

Jessica stood still. "Tony will think it's funny. Sophie, I'm going to be very embarrassed."

Sophie grabbed more marshmallows. "I need you to keep up with our job right now. We'll come up with a plan, a way to get to the other end of the enrober and be there when it comes out."

"Sorry." She set a row on the belt.

Uncle Sal called out, "Jessica, why don't you take my place here. Mr. Pleckenpoll can work next to Sophie."

Jessica began walking away, but leaned in and said, "If Emily doesn't notice my chocolate-covered jewelry, I might be okay. Think of a diversion."

At the other end of the enrober, Jessica copied Emily's actions by checking the tops and bottoms of each piece of candy to make sure they were covered. Any that weren't or had stuck together were set to the side. All the while, Jessica's nerves stretched tighter and tighter. The time inside the cooling area should end in a minute or two for her bracelet.

Uncle Sal stood near Sophie, and Jessica saw her cousin speaking with him. A few seconds later, he took Sophie's place, and Mr. P. hurried in Jessica's direction, at least he seemed to be hurrying for an old man.

He said, "Emily, I'm here to take over for you."

The woman stepped to the side. "It's all yours. These smell so good that I'm excited about those samples Sal mentioned." She headed toward Uncle Sal as the bracelet rolled out, along with many marshmallows, now completely covered in chocolate. Jessica grabbed it and stuffed it into her pocket as smoothly as she could, hoping no one had seen her. She sneaked a peek at Mr. P.

He raised an eyebrow. "A snack for later?"

Knowing her face had to be bright red, she lifted her bracelet up and barely out of her pocket. "My bracelet fell onto the enrober."

He chuckled. "That could be embarrassing. Your secret is safe with me."

Whew! Mr. P. understood.

Sophie came over to work with Mr. P., so Jessica stepped to the side. Then Uncle Sal left the marshmallow loading area to Dylan and his mother after they'd watched for a minute, and he headed their way.

"Did you get a good idea of what this machine can do?" Uncle Sal asked her, Sophie, and Mr. P.

Jessica glanced at Sophie and saw that her cousin was fighting laughter. Mr. P. was grinning. A bracelet that could pass as dessert probably fit in the category of something Uncle Sal *didn't* know the machine could do. He took over for Sophie, leaving her and Jessica to watch.

Jessica whispered, "I'm going to go to the restroom to get this out of my pocket before it's had time to melt. Or melt more than it already has."

"I'll walk with you," Sophie replied. "I want to tell you about something I saw."

They told Uncle Sal that they were going to the ladies' room and went on their way.

Once they reached it, Sophie checked under the stall doors to make sure no one was there while Jessica used hot water to rinse off her bracelet.

Sophie said, "Something strange happened right before we left. Mr. P. dropped a chocolate-covered marshmallow and bent over to pick it up."

"So?" Jessica ran a paper towel under the water, then wiped chocolate out of her pocket. The paper towel came out *almost* clean.

"He moved like a young man, much faster than he usually moves."

After checking her hair in the mirror and deciding it was fine, Jessica turned toward Sophie. "Maybe he felt young today."

"When he glanced my direction and saw me

watching him, he grabbed his side and made a small moan."

Jessica noted this as something to tell Sheriff Valeska. She'd said to remember anything odd. "I don't know why he'd do that. Keep watching him."

Sophie nodded. "I'm going to. Now, we'd better get back."

When they stepped out the door, Jessica saw a shadow around the corner. It stayed there a moment before moving away. Had someone followed them there?

5

The First Suspect

Back in the factory, Jessica watched everyone as they worked. No one looked suspicious. They all seemed to be who they said they were. But according to the sheriff, one of these people in the class or someone working here could be a spy.

When Jessica had checked her email on Uncle Lucas's computer the night before to see if she'd received anything from her parents who were in another country for her father's work, she'd also searched for information on people who stole secrets from businesses. It was called *industrial espionage*, she'd learned, because it involved a business—or industry—and those people were spying.

So, now she was looking for a spy. Not only that, but she was also a spy herself, because what else could you call someone who was watching people for the sheriff? She was a spy looking for a spy, and the worst part of it all was that she couldn't tell Sophie.

At the end of the class, Uncle Sal gave each of the

students a box with four pieces of chocolate in it. Dylan's mother immediately put both of theirs in her purse. Jessica suspected he wasn't going to get a bite of it.

Now she wondered what to do. She was supposed to watch everyone here and not get in trouble. But what if no one did anything suspicious in class but waited until afterward? How could she catch them? The only way she could think of was to follow them and see if they were who they said they were. That would be easier if Sophie knew what was going on. Jessica would have to be sneaky, and she didn't like that.

As everyone gathered the things they'd brought with them, Jessica pulled Sophie aside, while keeping her eyes on her classmates.

"Sophie, since we don't have a mystery, why don't we get some practice and pretend? Let's follow someone. We can improve our tailing skills."

Sophie's mouth dropped open. "That's the sort of thing I would suggest, but you always try to talk me out of it."

Jessica couldn't argue with the truth. "You're right, but it will give us something to do. And your mom isn't expecting us for a little while, right?"

"Right. Let's follow whoever leaves next."

Sophie grabbed her backpack and Jessica picked up her purse as Emily went out the door. They waited a minute, pretending that they were interested in pictures of chocolates on the wall, before leaving.

By now Emily was at the top of the hill that led down to Sweet Bites Chocolates. Jessica knew they didn't need to hurry though because a thick forest was on both sides of the street, and she'd already passed the old, overgrown road that led to the shore. Unless Emily decided to go through the woods, which seemed unlikely because she wasn't dressed for a hike, she had to continue on the road toward town.

Sophie said, "Let's keep our distance but keep her in sight."

Jessica was glad to have Sophie along. Her cousin knew how to be a detective.

"Do you know anything about her, Jessica? I only know her name."

Jessica had been paying more attention than she usually would. She'd always liked people, and she was interested in their stories, partly because she enjoyed writing, but this morning she'd tried to hear everything everybody said. "Only that she's visiting Pine Hill right now."

"Well, that's something anyway. I didn't recognize her. But why would someone take a class and stay inside when they came to a place like Pine Hill?

Jessica laughed. "Maybe she's like me and would rather be shopping."

"But she can shop and do inside things like that anywhere. Why here?"

"Excellent question, Sophie. We'll see if we get an answer by following her."

Having reached the top of the hill themselves, they watched Emily take a right turn on the first street she came to. Sophie walked faster. "We'd better speed up." The trees thinned out, and old brick houses started to appear beside the road. Every building in Pine Hill except the chocolate factory and Sophie's house was brick, as far as Jessica could tell.

Most of the town was to the right, including the downtown area, the beach, the marina and, if you walked far enough, Sophie's house. The only place Jessica remembered going to the left was the cemetery. And she hoped she'd never have to go there again.

When they turned onto another road with houses, this time with large trees overhanging the sidewalk, Emily was far ahead of them, but they could still see her.

"Whew! I'm glad she didn't go into one of those houses, or we would have lost her." Sophie did everything in a big way, including a pretend trailing of a pretend suspect. Jessica did hope that Emily was in the clear because she liked her.

"This is kind of fun," Sophie said.

Emily turned right. "I feel like a real detective right now, Jessica. Thank you! I'm not missing mysteries as much. But we'll have to be careful who we follow."

"Does that mean we plan on following more people?" Having Sophie on board with her spying was a very good thing.

"I'd like to. Maybe tomorrow we can tail one of the other people in the class."

Jessica laughed. "Maybe Mr. P., but he's old enough that I don't think he's going to get into trouble."

"I would guess that there are criminals who are young and some who are very old. But you're right. Mr. P. seems like a nice guy. I'd like to have him as a grandfather."

Toward the end of the street, Emily stopped. Sophie and Jessica darted behind one of the trees, which had fortunately been there as long as the houses had and was big enough around to hide the two of them. The girls peered around the tree, one of them on each side.

"She just stopped to tie her shoe," Sophie said. "Now she's on her way again."

They watched her turn the next corner toward what Jessica was pretty sure was the marina, the place where all of Pine Lake's boats were kept.

When they got to the corner, Emily was still ahead of them and in plain sight. By the time the marina came into view, woods lined the road again.

"I'm glad Emily's still moving because I don't see anything to hide behind here, do you, Sophie? She'd see us if we ran toward the forest."

"Very true. We have to move fast if we need to find a hiding place."

When they reached the marina, Emily suddenly stopped. Jessica couldn't tell why until she sat down on a bench, one of many that were scattered about on Pine Hill's wide sidewalks. She reached into her bag, pulled out a book, and opened it.

"Soph, we need to find a place to hide and in a hurry. She could easily look up from her book and see us standing here."

Sophie turned in a circle. Halfway around, she said, "Over here! Behind this trash can."

"Sophie, anyone who walks by or drives past us is going to think it's crazy for two girls to be crouched behind a trash can."

"Right." She continued around the circle. "Plan B: there's another bench that we passed a minute ago. If we sit on it, we'll be far enough away from Emily that she probably won't notice us, but we'll still be able to keep an eye on her. Better?"

"Much better. And much more comfortable too."

As they sat down on the bench a couple of minutes later, Jessica wished they had brought a book, as Emily had. "She could sit there for hours."

"Tomorrow, we can bring books, and I'll bring a little notebook to write in so we can take notes. What we learn about tailing people could be useful if we ever discover another mystery."

Jessica hoped they weren't in the middle of one right now. If the secret came out, would Sophie ever forgive her for not telling her?

"How much time do we have before we need to be at Great Finds?"

Sophie checked her watch. "We have about

twenty-five minutes. I'd like to learn more about Emily today so we can tail someone else tomorrow."

Emily rose to her feet when a boat came in, one that Jessica recognized as belonging to Captain Jack, the man who had taken them fishing once. Smiling from ear to ear, Emily closed her book and put it back in her bag. Then she walked slowly over toward the boat, which was pulling up into its spot at the dock.

Jessica and Sophie got up and walked closer.

A man waved to Emily from the boat. Once it had stopped, he jumped onto the dock. She ran into his arms, and he swung her up in the air. Captain Jack stepped off the boat and tied it up. Just when Jessica thought she and Sophie had gotten away cleanly without Emily noticing them, Captain Jack saw them and waved. He shouted, "Hello, lassies."

Sophie whispered to Jessica, "Pretend we've been out on a walk. Act casual."

They hurried over to his boat.

"What are you lassies up to on this fine summer morning? Any more mysteries?"

Sophie laughed, but Jessica could tell that it wasn't her real, happy laugh.

"We're taking a chocolate class right now," Sophie answered for both of them. "Emily is in it too. Jessica and I had a little bit of time before we had to get over to her mom's shop, so we were walking around."

Jessica bit back a grin. It was the absolute truth. They *were* walking around.

The man with his arm around Emily, said, "You're in the class with my wife?"

Emily nodded. "We had fun today, didn't we, girls?"

"We did. Your husband should have been there too."

He shook his head. "No! I'm here to fish. Emily doesn't like to fish, but she's happy to read a book. I was happy when she found out about the chocolate class because that was an extra special thing for her to do. We both get a vacation that we love."

"Jessica, it's time for us to get over to Mom's shop." To Emily, she added, "My mom owns Great Finds, the antique store on Main Street. If you get tired of reading, you can stop by."

"I may do that."

The girls waved good-bye and hurried away.

6

I See You

At Great Finds, Sophie stopped in front of the glass window facing the sidewalk. "Look," she said.

"At what?" Jessica asked. "Your mom has quite a few things in the window."

Sophie rolled her eyes. "How many of them could be used to solve a mystery?"

Only one stood out. "The spyglass."

Sophie nodded. "Exactly." She pushed open the door to Great Finds and saw her mother dusting. "That's your least favorite job at Mom's shop, isn't it, Jessica?"

"Yes. But it's easy to do. It seems to go on forever though when I'm doing it."

"Maybe she's already taken care of most of it." She went over to where her mother swept the feather duster over some teacups. "Mom! When did you get the spyglass?" Sophie pointed toward the window.

Mrs. Sandoval smiled widely. "I wondered how long it would take for you to notice. You do have good powers of observation. I can see that's a skill that has helped you solve mysteries. To answer your question, I bought the brass spyglass when I was at an event last spring, and it arrived today. Would you like to see it?"

Sophie didn't even speak up because she was sure her mother already knew the answer. They followed Mrs. Sandoval over to the window, where she took it out and set it in Sophie's hands.

Sophie held up the spyglass and aimed it toward the window. "This is great!" She scanned the street through the lens.

"Mom, the moon is pretty full right now, isn't it?"

"It is. You know your dad loves astronomy, and I remember him saying the other day that it was almost a full moon again."

"So there would be enough light even at night to see through a spyglass. This would be a good night to go camping, wouldn't it?" Sophie smiled brightly at her mother. "The place where we found the briefcase with the feathers has an amazing view of the lake."

"Wouldn't it be just as good to see the moon from your house, Sophie?" Jessica asked.

Sophie shook her head. "It would be more fun to watch the moon from a great spot like that one above Pine Lake."

Her mother chewed on her lip. "It seems safe. You haven't managed to get yourself in the middle of a mystery for weeks." She paused. "There are two of you and that's safer."

Jessica said, "I don't want to go camping, Sophie."

"It's you *and* Jessica or not at all," Mrs. Sandoval said to Sophie.

Sophie groaned and turned to Jessica. "Please?"

"Okay," Jessie agreed, but Sophie could tell she still didn't want to go. "I didn't think I would ever go camping in my whole life."

"Thank you!"

"Sophie, I do have that favor to ask of you," Mrs. Sandoval said. "Remember how I mentioned the choir to you two or three weeks ago?"

Not the choir! Sophie nodded very slowly.

"If you would go and sing—"

"No! Please, Mom, I'm a mystery solver, not a choir singer."

"All I'm asking is that you give it a try. Go once or twice and see if you like it. You have a very pretty voice when you sing at church." Her mother held out her hand.

Sophie stared at it. Then she reached for her mom's hand and shook it. "Deal. I sing twice?"

Her mother nodded.

"And I get to go camping tonight?"

"You aren't far from home when you're there. I think it should be okay. I'll have to see if your father agrees, but I believe he will."

"And we can take the spyglass?" As much as Sophie wanted it, she didn't think her mother would allow that.

"You can take it."

Sophie blinked, not sure she'd heard correctly. Her mother was always very careful with antiques, so why wasn't she worried about this one?

Jessica solved the mystery. "Aunt April, I noticed that the spyglass has a dent in the side. It isn't as perfect as most of the other things you have in your shop."

"Very observant. I bought it thinking that one day I might sell it, but since the spyglass isn't perfect, it isn't as valuable. I've decided to let Sophie use it for a while."

"Really? More than one night?" Sophie held it close to her chest. Then she said, "This has been a day of great things. Uncle Sal let each of us choose a piece of chocolate this morning. And he gave us each a box with four more pieces."

Mrs. Sandoval said, "Uncle Sal? Do you mean Salvatore Donadio?"

Jessica said, "He said that we're friends with Tony, and friends are like family to the Donadios, so we should call him Uncle Sal."

Mrs. Sandoval said, "That's fine. But Sophie, you've always said you did not like chocolate. You do now?"

Sophie tapped the counter as she thought about the answer. "The milk chocolate with the orange filling tasted good. At least, it wasn't bad."

Her mother and Jessica laughed.

Sophie said, "I've had enough chocolate for today. Jessica, let's not take any chocolate tonight. Okay?"

"That's fine with me. I know I get to eat more at the next class."

"It's time to pack for our night." Sophie walked toward the door, her hand securely around the spyglass.

7

It's a Mystery!

The shop door closed behind Sophie before Jessica could even get there. The last words she heard from her were from her list of things to take that night: ". . . tent, sleeping bags, food for dinner and breakfast, flashlights . . ." Jessica caught up with Sophie about half a block away. She certainly didn't want to waste any time in getting home to pack for this camping trip.

Once they were back at Sophie's house, her cousin packed swiftly. She asked her father to help haul some of their gear to the campsite, and faster than Jessica would have thought possible, they were alone in the woods beside a tent.

"This summer has been full of firsts." Jessica glanced around them. It was beautiful up here in a rustic, old-fashioned way. She and Sophie sat on some lightweight chairs, watching the sun set as they ate dinner. Jessica took a bite of her sandwich and chewed slowly, all the time playing the scene in her mind over and over again of Sheriff Valeska asking her to keep her eyes open at the chocolate factory.

She didn't need to worry here, though. They were a long way from Sweet Bites Chocolates. And the sheriff didn't say anything scary was happening. She said for Jessica to keep her eyes open, so it was probably safe to be in the woods.

Of course, there was the time when she and Sophie had first met, and Sophie had said there were wild animals up here, but Jessica still hadn't seen one. She hoped they were safe from those too. She glanced around as she ate the last bite of her sandwich. Their first mystery had begun with a clue they'd found up here.

The idea of clues sent her thoughts right back to Sweet Bites. There might not be anything strange happening inside that chocolate factory. Sure, there'd been that shadow that went around the corner this morning, but that could have a simple explanation, like one of the people who worked there stopped for a moment.

Jessica swallowed hard. "We're safe. We're safe," she said very low so Sophie wouldn't hear her.

"Are you okay, Jessica?"

"Sure. I'm fine. Absolutely wonderful." She laughed in a way that she hoped sounded real but didn't to her own ears.

A flashlight came on and shined in her direction. "You don't sound okay. Are you nervous about camping?"

Jessica held up her thumb and forefinger a short distance apart. "Maybe a little." She moved her hands so they were about a foot apart. "Maybe more than a little."

"Don't worry. I've camped up here lots of times. We're fine." Sophie took another bite of her sandwich. A minute later, she added, "Turkey sandwiches and watching the sun set over Pine Lake. This is awesome. I brought apples for dessert."

Jessica pointed at her braces, then realized Sophie couldn't see her. "Is mine cut up?"

"Of course. I know it's hard for you to eat apples otherwise." Sophie handed her a plastic bag with the apple in it.

Munching on an apple slice, Jessica realized this place was safe. She only had to worry about possible spies at the chocolate factory. No problem. No problem at all.

Heavy clouds early in the day had moved on, leaving a mostly clear sky. The stars shone overhead, and a full moon cast a bright light onto the lake in front of them, making it seem almost like daytime.

Sophie held up her spyglass and scanned the horizon.

"Is there anything out there?"

"Only water surrounded by pine trees. This is the first time I've used this away from town, and I wanted it to be interesting, maybe even exciting."

"That's a lot to ask for with a lake."

"Especially when we aren't working on a mystery."

Jessica *wasn't* working on a mystery, at least she hoped not. "I think Pine Lake's going to be quiet at night. Can I try the spyglass?"

Sophie handed it to her. "Let me know if you see anything. I'm going to relax and enjoy being out here in nature."

Right, nature. Where was a mall when you needed one? Jessica held up the spyglass and saw the lake through the circle at the end. Motion at the edge of the circle caught her attention, so she shifted it that direction. A little sailboat slowly moved toward the center of the lake.

"Hey Sophie, there's a boat."

"Really? Where?" Sophie reached for the spyglass and held it up, peering through it in the direction Jessica pointed. "There is. It's coming from the far side of the lake. Why would anybody be in a boat at night? That seems kind of risky. What if there was a log or something like that in the water? You wouldn't see it at all."

Jessica could barely make out the boat without the spyglass, and might not have noticed it otherwise. When it slid into the moon's reflection on the water, she could see its sails a little more clearly. "Can I look again?"

"Sure." Sophie handed it back. "A sailboat is so quiet that we wouldn't have known it was there if we weren't camping tonight."

Jessica found the boat again. Then everything went

dark. She lowered the spyglass and discovered that a cloud had covered the moon. "I think we're done using this tonight. The clouds made it dark enough that this is hard to see through." *And it's a lot creepier.*

As Jessica listened for anything in the trees and brush around them, the cloud moved off, and the moon reappeared. She returned the spyglass to Sophie who immediately raised it to the view.

"The boat stopped in the middle of the lake. That doesn't make sense."

"Maybe they think the moon is pretty, like we do, and wanted to sit in the moonlight."

Sophie laughed. "That's probably true. You know how I almost always want to be solving a mystery."

Stillness came over their campsite. There was only the sound of crickets in the woods and a light breeze that ruffled her hair. This was actually kind of pleasant, and her spying job at the chocolate factory more like a bad dream.

Suddenly Sophie jumped to her feet. "Jessica! They dropped something over the side of the boat. Then they turned in a circle and started back to shore."

Jessica noticed a second tiny speck on the water coming from near town. "Sophie, over there!" Jessica tugged the spyglass in that direction so Sophie could see it better.

"What is going on? People in two boats want to go out and see the moonlight in the same place?"

Another cloud moved over the moon.

"No!" Sophie cried out. "Move, cloud, move!" She swept her hand to the side as if she could move the cloud that direction. The light began increasing as the cloud moved on. "The first boat is gone. Wait! I see a trail of water behind a boat going back to where I first saw it."

Sophie gave Jessica time with the spyglass. A minute later, Jessica said, "The second boat doesn't have sails. It went right to the spot or very close to where the other boat stopped, and they pulled something onboard. They must have picked up whatever the other boat threw overboard."

"This is very strange."

Knowing Sophie would want to see what was happening, she handed the spyglass back to her.

"Jessica, the first boat went to a part of the lake I don't know very well. It's way on the other side of Pine Hill—beyond that, even." Sophie swung the spyglass to the right. "The second boat isn't going toward the marina either, and that's where all but a few of Pine Lake's boats are kept. Hold it . . . that boat might be going in the direction of the chocolate factory."

"Oh no! There *is* a mystery. If the boat is from there—"

Sophie lowered the spyglass and turned toward Jessica. "What are you saying?"

Jessica needed a quick answer. "That old building feels like a mysterious place with all its wandering hallways."

"Now you're talking. We might have found another mystery." Sophie looked through the spyglass again.

Jessica watched the second boat as it trailed away in the direction of the last place she would want it to go, Sweet Bites Chocolates. Now, instead of having fun making candy, she might have ended up in the middle of a mystery again.

8

The Secret's Out

Sophie lay in her sleeping bag, zipped all the way up, and stared at the ceiling of their tent. She kept thinking about the boats they had seen, and she couldn't figure out a reasonable explanation for them to be there. It reminded her of watching a foot race when the baton was passed from one person to another, but then it made sense. What would someone drop in a lake at night?

Jessica tossed and turned beside her, so she didn't think she was sleeping either. Sophie rolled onto her side.

"Jessica?" Sophie said in a very low voice so she wouldn't wake her if she had nodded off. "Are you asleep?"

"We have a new mystery. How can I sleep when there's a new mystery? Plus, I'm out here in the woods, practically in the middle of nowhere, in a tent that can't protect me from anything. And I just realized that there isn't any way for me to take a shower when I wake up in the morning, so I don't know if you're going to get cranky Jessica or what."

"Whoa. I know mornings are definitely not your best time of day. Let's fix that problem by my being very quiet and not talking to you until you talk to me in the morning. I'll wait for you to let me know if you're cranky or not."

"That makes sense. Now, about the mystery—"

"The two boats were acting weird. I'll admit that. It seems like a mystery, but I'm not sure what it would be."

Jessica was silent for about a minute, so long that Sophie wondered if she'd fallen asleep after all. Then she spoke. "Sophie, didn't you say you thought the second boat went back toward the chocolate factory?"

"Well, it didn't go toward the marina. You've been there, so you know where that is."

"That's what I thought too," Jessica said in a voice that Sophie would have to call sad. But why would she care?

"There isn't much built on the shore in that area. I guess it's because the space used to be filled with the building Mom talked about."

Jessica was quiet again. Then she said, "Sophie, I need to tell you something now, but I don't want you to be mad at me. Please remember that I couldn't tell you before, and I shouldn't be telling you now, but I'm worried that all of this might be very important."

She paused so long that Sophie wondered if she'd

fallen asleep. Then she finally added, "Maybe I should talk to the sheriff first."

"What? After you said the first part, I really want to know what it is that you're talking about."

"Okay. I'm trying to remember exactly what Sheriff Valeska told me, what she asked me to do, and I think I've got it."

"Sheriff Valeska asked *you* to do something? Tell me."

"I'm trying. Wait a second." Jessica took a deep breath then continued, "I think this is close to what she said. 'Jessica, I'd like you to keep your eyes open when you're in the chocolate factory. Let me know if you see anything suspicious. Don't tell anyone else.'"

Sophie wasn't sure what to say. She felt hurt and angry—all of those emotions raced through her in a jumbled mess. "Why didn't she ask me too?"

"Oh, I forgot that part. She said she was worried that you would get too involved and might get into trouble. And you know that's happened before, Sophie, so it made sense to me. You're a good detective. You would have wanted to dig deeper, and I think she just wanted someone to watch out for anything strange."

"Okay. I guess I can understand. You wouldn't get into the middle of anything."

"Right."

"Did you see anything suspicious at Sweet Bites?"

"Well, I saw a shadow going by at the end of the

hall, like someone had been standing there listening. But that didn't have to mean anything."

"I need to keep my eyes open now." Sophie rolled over onto her back. "I think we'd better try to sleep, Jessica. Tomorrow might be a very busy day."

"I had a feeling you would say that."

"The first thing in the morning, we need to get out of here and go see the sheriff."

"Sophie, you know she'll say we don't have any evidence. We don't have any clues for her to follow."

"But I still think she needs to know. What those boats did was strange."

Jessica said, "You're right, Sophie. We do need to tell her. I can't think of a single logical reason for two boats to do what we saw."

The next morning, Sophie watched her cousin open her eyes but didn't speak to her.

"I think waking up in a tent is a good thing. I feel fine," Jessica said.

Sophie raised one eyebrow but still didn't say a word.

Jessica unzipped the bag and sat up. "Let's start our day."

Sophie also sat up. "Are you sure?"

"I'm sure. I'm ready to start this mystery. What do we do first, Sophie?"

"First . . ." Sophie let the thought trail off in a mysterious way.

"Yes?"

"First, we eat breakfast."

Jessica pushed Sophie's arm. "I could figure that one out. I remember that you put snack bars in the bag for breakfast, and we have bottles of water. Right?"

As they finished their snack bars, Sophie stood. "Let's get everything packed up here, carry what we can, and get to my house."

On the hike back down Cutoff Trail, Sophie said, "Jessica, how would you describe where the second boat came from?"

Jessica took a step to the left so that a bush wouldn't swipe across her leg. "I'm not sure. I remember from the day we were out on the lake fishing earlier this summer that the lake stretches a long way in that direction."

"I've given it a lot of thought, and I think it came from the farthest part of the lake. I suppose it could've gone along the edge of the lake for a while and then cut across, but at that moment it seemed to be coming from over there."

Sophie paused, then added, "I've lived here all my life, but other than going with my parents once when I was a little kid to visit a man who lived in a house over there, I've never been to that part of the lake. I sure wouldn't want to walk that far from town."

"Does the highway even go that way?"

"Sort of. There is no road on the opposite side of

the lake from Pine Hill, but the road does go around to the area where we think the boat came from."

They stepped out of the woods and into an open area with a stream. Sophie took off running and jumped across it. Jessica had always walked across it on the large stones dotting the stream.

Sophie clapped her hands. "You can do it! Getting wet is the worst that can happen."

Jessica took a few steps backward so she could get a running start, took a deep breath, and ran as fast as she could at that stream. When she reached the edge, she pushed off with her feet and sprang across, landing neatly on the other side. "I did it! I did it!"

Grinning, Sophie patted her on the back. "You're getting there. For a city girl, you're doing pretty good."

"You're going to have to visit me in London, England, so I can give you some of my city training."

"Deal. We'll have to see if we can talk Mom and Dad into that."

They continued the short distance to Sophie's house. There they each took showers to wash off their camping grime and were soon ready, but not as soon as Sophie would have liked because Jessica did have to do all of her morning routines.

"Today I can wear perfume since we don't have class. Please remind me not to again tomorrow!"

"Sure." Sophie shrugged. "At least I'll try. I don't wear scented things, so I don't think of it."

They went into the living room. The sound of a door opening behind them caused them to both turn around. Mr. Sandoval came down the hall from his home office.

"Sophie," he said, "I want to make sure you remember that your mother's birthday is tomorrow. I thought we could all go out to dinner."

"Sounds great, Dad."

"In case you've spent your allowance"—he gave her a look that said he assumed she had—"I set some money on your nightstand so you can buy your mom a small gift. Jessica's mom already sent something."

"You've been extra busy with work lately, Dad, haven't you?"

"I have. A large company asked me to review their records. I'll complete the project next week. For now, I'm back to work." He turned toward his office. "I'll see you ladies at dinnertime."

"That's so nice of him," Jessica said after he'd gone into his office and closed the door.

"It's probably because he knows we've had to spend money this summer while we've been solving mysteries." Sophie raced into the bedroom. When she returned, she said, "I may need to check my nightstand every day if Dad's going to set money there."

Jessica laughed. "I doubt that's going to happen very often."

Sophie picked up her backpack and tucked the money into a zipper pocket. "Ready?"

"I am. Let's go tell Sheriff Valeska what happened last night. And let's see if she gives us her usual answer: 'Acting suspicious isn't a crime.'"

9

Telling the Sheriff

When the cousins arrived in town, Sophie slowed down.

"Is something wrong?" Jessica asked her.

"Remember what's happened when we've tried to talk to someone else at the sheriff's office? I think we should only tell the sheriff and come back if she isn't here."

"I agree." Jessica had to tell the sheriff that she'd given away the secret to Sophie, and she hoped she wouldn't be upset.

They made their way to the sheriff's office. Sheriff Valeska was sitting in her chair at her desk. Her secretary, Clare, asked them what they needed. They'd had a little problem with her when she'd first started working here earlier this summer because she hadn't believed kids could solve mysteries. She'd learned from the sheriff that these kids could.

Sophie said, "We have something we need to discuss with the sheriff." Sophie sounded quite professional. Her words reminded Jessica of the way people spoke in some of the old black-and-white detective movies Sophie loved to watch.

The sheriff looked up from her computer, leaned back in her chair, and motioned the two of them over to her desk. "Sit, ladies," she said, pointing at one chair, then another. "What can I help you with today?"

They sat down, and Sophie leaned forward in her chair. "Sheriff, we saw something strange last night."

A puzzled expression crossed the sheriff's face. "Last night? At your house?"

Jessica said, "No, we were camping."

Sophie added, "We went up Cutoff Trail. It was almost the same spot where we found the first clue in our first mystery."

"Okay. Go on. That has a good view over the lake, so I'm curious."

Sophie described what they'd seen with Jessica throwing in a few things now and then that she'd noticed. When they finished, the sheriff was quiet for a few moments. Then she said, "That's very interesting, ladies. You think the second boat went toward the area of the chocolate factory?"

The girls nodded.

"But I remember Sal Donadio mentioning that he didn't have access to the boat storage area, that the area had been closed off years ago, and now it was only accessible through a trapdoor in the floor. He said there wasn't even a ladder there. They had to lower a ladder down through the hole when some plumbing needed to be repaired right after he bought the building."

"But where else would the boat have gone to, Sheriff? It didn't appear to be going in the marina's direction."

"I don't know, Sophie. I would say that maybe they went along the edge of the lake for a while, but I don't know a whole lot of people who would want to make a trip in a rowboat longer than it had to be. That's a lot of work."

"Sheriff . . ." Jessica leaned closer to the sheriff and said in a low voice, "I had to tell Sophie."

Sheriff Valeska glanced around the room. Clare was the only other one there. The sheriff must have decided she needed to tell them something that no one else should know because she said, "Girls, I want to show you something in our storeroom." She pushed back her chair, stood, and walked over to a door that led into a small room to the side of the larger office the sheriff and her deputies shared.

They followed her inside.

The sheriff kept the door open and spoke in a low voice. "Jessica, how much does Sophie know?"

"All of it, Sheriff. It was hard to keep it from her, and I thought that when we saw the boats, it might all connect. I hope you're not upset with me."

A silence stretched so long that Jessica thought the sheriff was angry. Then Sheriff Valeska said, "I'm not upset with you. Disappointed, maybe. But I might have done the same thing. I never should have kept Sophie out of the loop."

Sophie smiled. "Thank you, Sheriff. I thought maybe I'd done something wrong."

"No, Sophie. You tend to leap into things, and I didn't want you to get into danger. I knew Jessica wouldn't do that."

"Now that we've both been told, is there something we can help with, something *I* can help with?" Sophie asked with more than a little bit of excitement in her voice.

The sheriff gave Sophie a firm look. "Sophie, I don't want you in trouble. Do you understand?"

Sophie nodded. "I do, Sheriff."

The sheriff stood there and continued to give her that look.

"I promise, Sheriff," she added. "I will do my best to stay out of danger."

The sheriff sighed. "That's probably the best I can ask. Be safe, Sophie. And you too, Jessica. Don't let her drag you into anything she shouldn't. Call me first."

Sophie asked. "Did you ever find the stolen car?"

"No. We did not. It's one of the only cars ever stolen in this town, so that's strange too. Please be careful."

Jessica leaned toward the sheriff. "Do you have any more information to give me? You said to keep my eyes open, but I don't know for what."

The sheriff took off her hat and rubbed the top

of her head. "There's the possibility that something odd is going on at the chocolate factory. At least, that's what Sal Donadio thinks. He came up with what he believed was an idea for a new flavor of chocolate, and about a month later another company came out with the exact same thing. He brought me samples of both, and I couldn't tell the difference."

"So, someone is stealing secrets from the chocolate factory? There's a spy?" Jessica asked. She'd been right.

The sheriff laughed. "I wouldn't call it a spy, Jessica. I will say there is the possibility that someone has stolen a single recipe, but it might be a coincidence. Two companies might have thought pineapple with the same secret ingredient would work."

Jessica asked, "Secret ingredient?"

"That's right. Sal isn't saying what it is."

Sophie nodded. "That does make it odd that they taste the same."

Sophie and Jessica left the sheriff's office with her promising to send a patrol car out in the area of the houses at the far end of the lake. She would have them go there a couple of times every night to make sure nothing strange was going on.

Sophie stopped on the sidewalk in front of the building. "I'm frustrated, Jessica."

"The sheriff was nice about everything."

"You're right. But I still think that second boat

went to the area around Sweet Bites. The land dips down to the lake there. Then it goes up the hill to the big mansion. There isn't anything else around."

"I think we've done everything we can, Sophie."

"I have an idea."

"Am I going to like this idea?"

"Only one part of it. Let's go sit and talk about it."

Jessica knew where Sophie would go. They were soon sitting on the wooden bench on the sidewalk that her cousin liked to go to when she had to figure something out.

"I'm ready for your plan, Sophie."

Sophie wasted no time. "We need to see if there's a boat under the chocolate factory where boats used to be kept. And if there is one, whether or not it's a rowboat."

"That sounds impossible to me, Sophie."

"Sweet Bites is Tony's uncle's business. We can trust Uncle Sal—at least I hope so—but I don't want to tell him too much."

Jessica thought about it for a few seconds. "We believe he's trustworthy, but he might tell someone who isn't. I think too many people could find out if we asked Uncle Sal about checking under the boathouse."

"We need to bring Tony into this mystery now. If his nephew wanted to explore under there—"

"It would just seem like a kid who's curious. And people don't pay attention to kids all the time, do they? Genius!" Jessica laughed.

As they walked away, Sophie said, "I've been thinking about yesterday. We tailed Emily Foster because you were spying on everyone. Is that right?"

"I was." Jessica held up her hand to stop Sophie from saying more. And hopefully to stop her from getting angry. "But I could have gone by myself. I took you with me because I thought it would be good to have you there."

"So even though I didn't know I was in the middle of a mystery, I *was* in the middle of one. You found the mystery this time."

"Yes. Does that mean you aren't mad at me?"

"I'm working on it. I really am."

10

Bringing in Tony

Sophie and Jessica found Tony at Donadio's Deli, as expected. He stood behind the counter making sandwiches for a family.

They got in line behind one other person, then placed their orders for sandwiches. Jessica got a turkey on white, and Sophie a pastrami on rye bread. Sophie caught Tony's eye and gestured with her head toward the table where they would sit. His eyebrows shot up, and he gave a nod. Tony had been in on their last two mysteries, and she knew he would be up for another one.

She and Jessica seated themselves at one of the small tables.

"I'm glad we're here early," Jessica said.

"You're always glad when we're here," her cousin answered.

Jessica felt her face flush. "This time it's because I'm very hungry. That snack bar didn't last very long. Also, since we're here ahead of the lunch crowd, there isn't anyone behind us in line, and Tony can take a few minutes to sit with us."

A few minutes later he brought them their sandwiches, set them down in front of them, and pulled out a chair for himself. He leaned close and spoke in a low voice. "New mystery?"

Sophie laughed. "Maybe we just wanted to say hello to you."

Leaning back in his chair, he watched the two of them "You have your working-on-a-mystery look, Sophie."

Sophie shrugged. "You're right, Tony. Well, maybe there's a mystery. At least I think there's a mystery."

Tony gestured forward with his hand. "Give. What's going on?"

She explained about the boats, and Jessica jumped in to repeat what the sheriff had told her about the chocolate factory. Sophie added the story of their tailing Emily Foster.

Tony gave a low whistle. When he did that, his mother glanced his way. "I'd better hurry. The lunch crowd will arrive soon. You want me to talk to my Uncle Sal?"

"If you can."

"As long as I'm part of the mystery-solving team. My uncle comes in here for lunch every day at about one o'clock." Tony stood. "I never know what he'll order, and sometimes he combines things that are strange together."

Jessica laughed. "We've noticed that at the chocolate factory. He has some crazy ideas."

He leaned forward. "Like?"

"Chocolate-covered bubblegum," Jessica said every word slowly.

Tony grimaced.

"That's what everybody in the class thought. He isn't going to make it now, so he has a big stack of bubblegum in his storage room."

Tony laughed. "That probably means we'll get bubblegum in our stockings this Christmas. And I'm okay with that. I'll ask him when he comes in if we can explore under his factory. Does that sound good?"

"Yes. We'll be over at Great Finds, doing whatever it is Mom needs us to do this afternoon. That was our deal. She pays for the class, and we work." Sophie popped the last bite of her sandwich in her mouth.

Tony straightened. "You don't sound happy about that, Sophie."

She took a sip of her drink, then stood. "I don't mind working there. But right now, I don't think I want to take over the antique store when I'm grown up. You like being here in the deli. Maybe I'll change my mind when I'm older and be glad for all of the time I spent in Mom's shop. But maybe not." Sophie grinned.

"I'll call you at Great Finds this afternoon and let you know what I set up. When do you want to go?"

"I don't want too much time to pass from when we saw the boats to when we get in there."

"Makes sense. I'll ask about this afternoon."

Sophie and Jessica left and went to her mom's shop. When they got there, Mrs. Sandoval put them to work doing Jessica's favorite chore, unpacking boxes. After taking everything out of two boxes and carefully unwrapping each item, Jessica said, "I love this. It's like Christmas! I get to open packages with beautiful things inside, things that are from the past."

"I don't mind in the beginning, but we still have one more box to do. I'm ready to be finished with this. And what I really want is for Tony to call."

At that moment the phone rang. The two of them looked at each other. Mrs. Sandoval answered it, but instead of passing the phone to one of them, she picked up a pen and made some notes on a piece of paper.

Jessica's shoulders dropped. "That can't be him," she said in a low voice to Sophie.

They got back to work unwrapping and started on the last box. When they were almost done, the phone rang again. This time after Mrs. Sandoval answered it, she handed the phone to Sophie. "It's Tony for you."

Sophie took the phone and glanced at her mother, standing nearby. "Hey, Tony. What's up?"

She didn't want her mother to worry about their finding a possible mystery, so that meant she couldn't say much. She listened as Tony told her the same thing that Sheriff Valeska had, that there was no easy access to the underside of his uncle's building. "Okay."

Mrs. Sandoval picked up one of the pieces they had unwrapped and walked into the back room with it. Sophie whispered, "There must be a way to get into there."

Tony answered. "That's what I said. Uncle Sal told me that the only way he knew was from the lake. All we have to do is swim around the side of the building and underneath the big door that's there. He gave me permission to do that anytime I wanted and said my friends can come with me."

Jessica had gone in a boat with Sophie, and she loved being at the beach, but Sophie didn't know if she could swim. She motioned Jessica closer. "Can you swim?"

Jessica's eyes widened. "Sure."

"Tony, we can do it." She suggested a time and a place to meet in a couple of hours.

Tony agreed, and they hung up.

11

Swimming for Clues

A half hour later, the girls left the shop. After a fast trip to Sophie's house, they returned to town with their swimsuits on under their clothes and small towels stuffed into her backpack.

They took the road to the chocolate factory, then right before the factory, the turn to the lake that once led to the long-gone building her mother had told them about.

Tony waited for them on the shore with a ball and an inflated ring. "Uncle Sal doesn't think there is anything under his factory that's worth making an effort to see. He went in there in a boat before he bought the building, and he said it was an old, abandoned place where they used to keep boats. It isn't even connected to the rest of the building anymore, even though it must have been in the past."

All three of them took off their outer clothes and stood in their swim clothes. Sophie's bathing suit was a simple blue one-piece, the style that someone on a swim team would wear. Jessica's was also a one-piece but pink and had a ruffle across one shoulder. Tony wore black swim trunks.

Jessica looked up at the chocolate factory. "I hope no one sees what we're doing. The factory part only has high windows, but the offices have larger windows, and someone could watch us from them."

Tony followed her gaze. "Even if someone saw us go into the water, the windows aren't in a place where they can see us if we stay near the building. "

Sophie said, "Let's play in the water for a while so they'll think that's what we're here to do. Then we'll inch over closer to the building, and they'll assume we're still horsing around."

Sophie tossed the inflated ring toward Jessica, who caught it, and they all went into the water. Jessica leaned on the ring and floated. Sophie and Tony threw the ball.

Just as it started to seem like fun, Sophie realized they were about to go somewhere that was completely unknown and could possibly lead to danger. She threw the ball over Tony's shoulder, and he swam over there. He tossed it a few feet closer to the building, and Sophie swam to get it. Jessica paddled around in a circle that grew ever wider but more toward the direction they needed to go. Foot by foot they grew nearer to the side of the building.

While dogpaddling, Tony glanced up. "I'm sure they can't see us now. You ready to go in there?" He gestured toward the building.

Jessica let go of the inflatable, and Tony dropped the ball inside it. Sophie hoped they would still be there when they came back out. They all swam around the corner of the building and under the old wooden door that covered the lake side. It reminded her of a garage door.

As they dogpaddled in an open area, Tony said, "This isn't what my uncle described. Sure, some of this is old, but half the boards on the little dock in front of us are new wood."

They swam to that dock and climbed up a ladder that went down into the water. At the back, stairs led from the right side of the dock upward to the chocolate factory. The three of them peered over the side of the dock to a rowboat tied up there.

Jessica said, "Okay, Ms. Detective, there's a boat, but it's an old one. I don't think I'd want to be on the lake in it."

Tony pushed on it with his foot, and it rolled from side to side. "She's right. It's floating, but it seems pretty rickety."

Sophie saw a boat that seemed old but sound. "I don't know. If it's dry inside, that makes it a good boat, doesn't it?"

Jessica said, "How could we tell if it had been used?"

"It's empty, so it isn't offering any clues." Sophie

turned to check out the large, rustic boathouse. "Let's see if there are any clues in here. Spread out and look for anything unusual."

Tony said, "Your detective team obeys."

Sophie grinned. "Sophie's team. I like that."

Tony checked the back wall to the right of the stairs, Jessica the wall under the stairs, while Sophie stared at the stairs as she decided whether or not she should climb them.

Jessica interrupted her thoughts. "Team leader, this wall has old, cracked paint, so it's been here a while."

Sophie went over to see it. "That may be new wood that they've tried to make appear old. Mom once used paint that does that on something she bought for our house. You know Mom, she wants everything to be old." Walking back toward the stairs, Sophie decided she would try them.

When she stepped onto the first step, Jessica hurried over. "Sophie, what are you doing? Uncle Sal said we could be down here, but he didn't say anything about us going up into the factory."

"Actually, my uncle said we could explore. He didn't say where. Those stairs are in bad shape though."

Sophie went up a few more steps then stopped and studied the next step which had a large, rotten-looking section. She stared up at the top of the stairs. "There's a door. I'd like to see what's beyond it, if we can get inside."

"Uncle Sal made it sound like this area was sealed off years ago."

"You're probably right, Tony. The next step isn't in great shape. I don't think anyone has been here for a long time."

Jessica went to the side of the stairs where Sophie could see her. "They might not be safe! Please come down."

Even she wondered if she should go back down. She did want to see the top though. Sophie gently put first one then the other foot on the broken step. "I think it's okay. I'm standing on this one now. I can keep going."

As she shifted forward to take another step, the wood broke with a crash. When the wall moved swiftly by, she closed her eyes. She landed on her back on the dock. When she opened her eyes, she found wood piled around her and saw the splintered ruins of the staircase above her.

Jessica leaned over her. "Sophie, can you see me?"

"Yes. I'm fine now that I'm not falling anymore."

Tony picked up a piece of wood lying on her and set it to the side.

She took a deep breath, then sat up and rubbed her arm. "Other than a bruised elbow, I'm fine. I am very glad I was only halfway up so I had a short fall." She got to her feet. "I did prove that no one has used those stairs to get to the rowboat from the building."

Tony shook his head. "We might have found an easier way to do that."

Jessica kicked at a splintered piece of wood. "Maybe we should move away from the stairs, in case the whole staircase collapses."

"Good idea." Sophie took a few big steps.

Standing on the dock, Jessica said, "Why would someone repair the dock but not the stairs so they could go from the dock to the building above us?"

Tony walked the dock from side to side. "None of this makes any sense."

A clunk from above their heads made Sophie jump. "Whew. Someone must have dropped something in the factory."

Jessica glanced around nervously. "Sophie, the wood breaking and you falling made a loud crash. If we can hear them upstairs . . ."

Sophie hurried toward the ladder into the water. "We need to leave. Quickly. If there *is* a way in from the factory, someone could be here any second."

They swam back out, found the inflated ring and ball in almost the same place they'd left them, and went back to shore.

As they dried off, Jessica said, "Maybe we should tell Sheriff Valeska." She reached for her shirt and began dressing.

"You know what she'll say." Sophie, with her shirt on over her suit, straightened her shoulders and did her best imitation of the sheriff. "'There is no evidence that a law has been broken. It is private property.'"

Tony held his T-shirt in his hand. "I guess I should

tell my uncle that someone repaired the dock. But why would anyone do that?" He pulled on the shirt, then the shorts.

"Tony, we don't know why this happened or who did it. Maybe we should keep it as our secret while we investigate for a few days. His not knowing means he can't act differently around one of his employees, and he can't tell the wrong person about what we found. If he did, that might put him and all of us in danger."

"Our family is very close, and we tend to tell each other things, but I think you're right. Let's wait a few days, a week at the most. By the time the chocolate classes are over next week, we'll have figured it out, or we'll have to tell."

Tugging on her jeans, Sophie said, "Deal."

After Tony had left, Sophie said, "I think we can be positive now: we have another mystery."

"A repaired dock for an old rowboat *is* strange. It does seem to be a mystery."

"We need to be careful."

"I couldn't agree more, Sophie."

"We'll watch carefully every second when we're in the chocolate factory this week. Let's do everything we can to not let the criminals know that we've learned anything about their secrets. We don't know who could be one of the bad guys. Except for Tony's uncle."

"I'm glad someone's in the clear."

12

Sharing Suspicions

Sophie woke to the scent of bacon cooking. Jessica's covers were flipped back, and the shower was running. Moments after the water was turned off, Jessica came out of the bathroom, rubbing her hair with a towel.

"My shower helped, and I think I'm ready to face the day."

Sophie didn't say a word.

Jessica sniffed the air. "Is that bacon I smell?"

Sophie grinned. "That's something that would wake me up too." She scrambled out of bed, grabbed her robe, and slipped it on as she headed for the kitchen. She knew it would take her cousin a while to dry her hair, and her mother might want help with breakfast.

When she opened the kitchen door, Mrs. Sandoval was standing at the stove. She looked up and said, "Good morning. Sophie, please pour orange juice for everyone and set the table. Your dad's home this morning, and I know both you and he love pancakes."

A breakfast of pancakes and bacon was soon ready, a meal that Sophie always loved. Jessica joined them with her hair and makeup perfect and wearing a yellow and white shirt with yellow shorts. Sophie still had her robe on.

When everyone was seated, she asked, "Why the special breakfast, Mom?"

"I haven't gotten to spend time in the morning with you girls for a while, so I thought this would be a good thing to do."

"I feel the same way," Mr. Sandoval said. "What have you been up to?"

Sophie and Jessica glanced at each other. Jessica took a bite of pancake and gave Sophie a look that said it was her job to answer.

"We went swimming yesterday." Sophie bit into a piece of bacon.

After a sip of juice, Jessica added, "And we've been taking the chocolate-making class."

"Dad, we brought chocolates home. You can have some if Mom shares with you."

Smiling, he said, "I'll have to move fast, or they'll be gone."

Mrs. Sandoval leaned over and gave him a kiss on the cheek. "You will have to move very quickly."

"Speaking of chocolate, Aunt April, I noticed that your house is wood outside, and so is the chocolate factory. But everything else I've seen in Pine Hill is made of brick. You know Pine Hill's history well. Do you know why?"

"Jessica, there's a reason for that. The chocolate factory and our house were built by the same builder. He must have preferred wood."

Mr. Sandoval picked up his cup of coffee, stood, and said, "I'll let you solve Pine Hill's past mysteries. I need to get back to my office." He headed for the kitchen door and left.

Mrs. Sandoval stood. "Please come about noon, and you can go to the deli before working. I'll give you money for that, of course. I have a project for you. This may be one you don't like."

With that, she sailed out the door.

Sophie said, "That doesn't make me look forward to this afternoon."

"Me either. But we've already cleaned out her storeroom, dusted, and unpacked boxes of new things for her shop. Maybe she said that to tease you."

"I guess that's possible. But Mom doesn't usually do that."

After the two of them did the dishes, Sophie went to take a shower and get ready. When she was dressed, she stepped out of her bedroom and found Jessica reading a book in the living room and her mother adding a book to an already tall stack of books that were crowded onto a small table against the wall.

"Mom, what's all that?" Sophie stepped over to the stack. Behind the books lay two, big rolled-up tubes of papers with rubber bands holding them in place and a small, old box.

"The library has decided to have a Pine Hill history room. It was just a meeting room, but now there will also be shelves with things like these. The box is filled with love letters from someone who lived here a long time ago. I found those when I was asked to go in and give values for the items in a house that was going to be sold."

Mrs. Sandoval tapped the rolls of paper with her finger. "One of those is the plans the architect drew for our house. The other is the plans for a large house on the far side of town."

Sophie twisted them and found the one with her address. "Can I open this?"

"Sure. I've never taken the time to truly study the drawings. I doubt you'll find any surprises."

Jessica came over as Sophie rolled out the plans on the dining room table. "Check this out. Here's my room. Correction: our room for the summer." Sophie pointed to that spot on the drawing.

"Sophie, you already know this house inside and out."

Mrs. Sandoval said, "That's what I think too, Jessica. But you know Sophie. She has to look. In addition to the chocolate factory, the man also built the building that was beside it. I think there's a photo of both of them in this old book about Pine Hill."

She went through the stack beside her, pulled out the fattest book, and flipped through it. "Here." She held the book open, and a beautiful building stared out at them. It was like many of the old houses in town, but fancier than any she'd seen with decorations all over it.

"The factory is simpler and reminds me of our house."

"Yes. The builder lived in this house for years." Mrs. Sandoval gathered the stack of books in her arms. "I need to get to the shop."

Sophie stared at the pages in front of her. "I'd like to study these plans."

"Sure. I'll take them next week. See you ladies at lunchtime."

After Mrs. Sandoval had left, Sophie said, "The drawing of the first floor shows everything as it is."

Sophie flipped the page to show the drawing of the second-story.

Jessica circled her finger around one area. "What's this?"

Sophie shrugged. "It's the closet in our guestroom."

"No, I mean in the closet." Jessica tapped the spot on the drawing. "If those lines show the closet, what is this?"

Sophie leaned in closer. "There are dashed lines on the drawing behind that closet, but not behind my parents' closets." She flipped the page back to where it showed her room on the first floor. "And not with my closet. But there are a few tiny dashed lines in my closet, and I know that's . . ." Sophie's jaw dropped, and her eyes slowly rose to meet Jessica's.

"That's my hiding place under a floorboard in the closet. If dashed lines mean there's a secret hiding place"—she flipped back to the closet in the guestroom—"then this might be a larger hiding place. Let's very carefully go over every part of the drawing to see if anything else has those lines."

After studying the attic's drawing, Jessica said, "The attic doesn't have anything like that." Flipping through the stack, she added, "I don't see the basement's drawing here."

"We'll figure that out later. Let's go!" Sophie headed for the staircase.

"I don't have to ask what you're planning to do." Jessica laughed.

Sophie heard Jessica's footsteps on the stairs behind her. Once in the guestroom, Sophie pushed aside hanging clothes and stepped into the closet.

"This is filled with old clothes."

"It's our winter coats and warm clothes," Sophie answered. "When we actually have a guest stay in this room, we clear the closet, but otherwise this is where Mom has us put all of those things." She rubbed her hand over the wall, and a line down the middle stopped her. "Jessica, feel this."

Sophie stepped to the side so Jessica could squeeze into the closet with her.

"There." Sophie gestured toward the area, and Jessica rubbed her hand on it.

"You may have found something, Sophie."

Sophie stepped over to the wall and tapped on it with her knuckles. "It sounds hollow."

"Would you know if something sounded *hollow*?"

"They say that a lot in mystery books. I can only say that it doesn't sound like there's a hard wall there."

"If it opens, there has to be a hinge, and if the only opening is in the middle, then the hinge must be on one of the two corners where the back wall meets the sides. Maybe a flashlight would help, Sophie."

"Good idea. I know there's one downstairs in a kitchen drawer for when the power goes out." Sophie hurried out the door. She returned quickly with a flashlight in her hand and pushed the button to turn it on as she entered the room. Then she stepped into the closet and held it up close to the line in the middle and checked both sides of the wall.

"Excellent idea, Jessica. The left side is solid. The wood there is very tightly put together, but the right side has a slightly wider opening. It's tiny, but it's there." She handed Jessica the flashlight so she could see it too.

"That means either the middle or the side has door hinges, Sophie. Maybe we need to push along both of the openings to see if we can find the right spot to have it open. If there is a door and if it opens that way. Those are really big *ifs*."

Sophie gave the upper corner a push, and the right side of the back of the closet swung back.

"Not anymore."

13

Watch Your Step

Jessica shined the flashlight into the opening in the back of the closet. A spiral staircase made of stone wound down and into darkness. "I bet we'll find a creepy basement, and I had enough of those with our first mystery. Rats live in basements!" She shuddered.

"Remember this is *my* basement. It's where our washer and dryer are. I've been in my basement hundreds of times, and I know there aren't any rats in it."

"That does make it more appealing. But have you ever seen the other end of this staircase?"

Sophie took the flashlight from Jessica and shined the light all the way around the opening. "No. I haven't. Let's find out where it goes." Sophie took a step toward it.

Jessica put her hand on her arm to stop her. "Maybe we shouldn't go down the stairs alone."

"I think it's safe. No one is down there."

Jessica stepped in front of her. "Let me go first. I'm the guest here, so I won't get in as much trouble as you for exploring without your parents being here." The rough texture of the stones with the mortar in between them gave her something to hold onto as she stepped onto the first step.

As she took a second step, a spiderweb caught in her hair and covered her hand. "Ick! Sophie, there are more spiderwebs here than I have ever seen in my life!"

"I'll get the broom from the kitchen. Maybe we can sweep the air in front of us." Sophie rushed from the closet.

While Jessica waited with webs around her for what seemed like an hour, she hummed her favorite song, a happy one to take her mind off all of the spiders living here who had spun the webs. Sophie returned and passed her the broom. Jessica held it up in front of her and swept down all the webs as she thought, *I won't see any spiders here.* She followed the steps downward as far as the broom had been able to reach, then swept it through the air again to clean another stretch of stairs before continuing.

A voice in the distance behind her said, "Do you see anything?"

"Just more stairs. I'm still going down."

"I guess I'd better follow you."

A scuffling sound came from behind Jessica, and she was glad to know it was Sophie and not a fat rat. Finally, Jessica arrived at the bottom of the stairs.

She shined the light in front of her. A room the size of Sophie's bedroom lay before her.

Sophie stepped beside her on the last step.

"There's a desk. It looks like an office, don't you think, Jessica?"

"But why would someone have a hidden office?"

"Well, my dad always says it's hard to get work done with people around. That's why he likes to work from home. Maybe the builder found a way to fix that."

Rolls of drawings like the one that had revealed this staircase were stuffed in one container. A desk, but with a top that slanted at an angle, was off to the side. A long table sat in the center of the room. Sophie walked over to the rolls of papers, pulled one out, and stretched it out on the table. "Bring the flashlight over here, Jessica."

Jessica did as she'd asked and shined the light on the unrolled paper.

"This is for a house on a street where we trailed Emily," Sophie told her. She checked another, then one more. "They're all for houses in Pine Hill."

Jessica took out a set of drawings. "This roll of papers is different, bigger than the others." When she unrolled it and shined the light on it, she said, "It's for the chocolate factory—I mean, the boat-house. Let's see if there's anything usual on it."

Page by page, they flipped through the plans for the building.

"Here." Sophie grabbed the flashlight from Jessica

and held the light over it. Then she circled an area with her finger.

Jessica leaned over. "Dashed lines."

Sophie nodded slowly. "We may have found another secret passage." She stood up straight, tucked the flashlight under her arm, and rolled up the papers.

"I think we'll need Tony's help again," Jessica said. "Uncle Sal will have to give us permission to search for it."

"I agree. We'll ask Tony at lunch. I hope he's there today."

Jessica turned in a slow circle. No door was in sight. "I wonder if there's a way to get out of here. I mean, other than the staircase. Shine the light over here on this wall. The left side is the foundation of the house, but the right side should be your basement."

Sophie shined the light as Jessica suggested. "It looks like a solid wall to me. But I have an idea. Jessica, if it was dark in here and light in the basement we might be able to see light coming through a crack. We'd know there's a way out or at least a place we should check to see if it's a way out."

"That sounds like a great idea."

"I'll go out, turn the light on in the basement, and come back here." She handed the flashlight back to Jessica and went back up the steps.

Jessica continued to scan the walls while Sophie

was gone but couldn't see anything. This whole place didn't make sense.

When her cousin returned and was safely beside her, Jessica turned off the flashlight, sending them into complete darkness.

After their eyes had adjusted, light trickling under the wall caught their attention. Without speaking, the two of them hurried over and felt around on that wall. Jessica tried pushing, twisting, and turning everything she touched. A snap sounded, and the door swung outward, letting in light from the basement.

Sophie asked, "How did you open it?"

Jessica moved a small piece of wood to the right and left. "I happened to put my hand on the right thing, I guess. The bigger question is why you and your family never noticed that the basement wasn't as big as it should be."

They stepped out into the basement itself.

Sophie said, "We're on the opposite side of the room from where the laundry is done, and that's the only part of it we use very often. And the basement itself is kind of an odd shape. I guess it never seemed strange. This was back in a dark corner."

Turning back to face the once-hidden room, Jessica shined the flashlight toward the ceiling. Two very old-fashioned lights hung there. "I wondered how the builder was able to see and work in here." Jessica stood on a chair so she could see the lights up close. "These are so old-fashioned that they're gas lamps. When the house was first built, I guess it had gas flames for light."

"Come out into the basement, Jessica." When she had, Sophie pushed the newly discovered door shut. "I don't see how to open it from here, so we can close the closet's entrance from upstairs." She turned toward the basement stairs. "I'm surprised at all of this. I checked for secret passages in this house a long time ago."

"Not many people can say that, Sophie."

Sophie laughed. "I spent a lot of time around the fireplace because there are often secret places there, at least in books. But I never checked closets. That surprises me because after reading *The Lion, The Witch and the Wardrobe*, you would think I would have immediately checked all the closets. Anyway, I never found anything before today."

As they came up the stairs, Sophie glanced at her watch. "Oh no! Jessica, we have to hurry to get to Great Finds. We'll close the door in the closet later."

They hurried out the door and toward town at a pace somewhere between walking and running. The girls arrived on time but panting.

When they'd caught their breath, they went into the antique shop. Mrs. Sandoval stood at the cash register with a customer, so they went to the other side of the shop and waited. When the customer left, Mrs. Sandoval handed them some money. "Have fun at lunch. I'll have you help me rearrange some things when you come back."

As they left, Jessica said, "That doesn't sound bad to me."

Sophie shrugged. "Me either. Maybe it's something Mom doesn't enjoy."

"Your mother's been very nice to us. We work and she pays us, and we get to have lunch out. I like that."

"You'd like it even if she didn't pay us because she keeps letting us go to the deli. Aren't you getting tired of it?"

"I did for a little while. But then I started having a different sandwich every time I went, or soup. There's so much to choose from that I'm not tired of it anymore. Besides, we usually see Tony there."

When they arrived, they placed their orders. While they waited at a table, Sophie said, "Jessica, we need to share about what we found today with Tony."

"Agreed. I've also been thinking about another way Tony might be able to help us." At Sophie's curious expression, she added, "This must be the most popular place to eat lunch in Pine Hill. He sees many of the people who live here and visit."

Right then, he brought their sandwiches. Glancing around first, he then leaned close and spoke in a low voice. "Anything new on the mystery?"

Jessica said, "Yes and no. First, I have a question. The other students in the class are suspects. We followed Emily Foster, and she seems okay. I don't think we'll find anything unusual about Dylan, other than the fact that his mother may be driving him a little crazy sometimes."

"Is there anyone else in class?" Tony asked.

Sophie spoke. "Mr. Pleckenpoll. He said we could call him Mr. P."

"Oh yes, the friendly old man. He eats at the deli most days."

"I saw him move more like a young man once, so I'm watching him. Tomorrow we'll follow him."

Tony glanced from Sophie to Jessica. "You've learned something, haven't you?"

"It might be easiest if Tony came to my house tonight so we could show him what we found."

With a serious expression on his face, Tony asked, "What might be easiest? Are you getting me in the middle of a mystery again?"

Jessica hesitated. She'd thought that Tony liked being part of their mysteries. He'd seemed happy when they swam under the boathouse. "Yes, we were. But if you don't want to be involved, we totally understand." She looked nervously over at Sophie, who also wore a concerned expression.

Tony grinned. "Just kidding. I wouldn't want to miss a second of a mystery."

"Not funny." Sophie pushed on his arm. "Do you think you can be at my house at seven o'clock tonight?"

"It will have to be earlier than that. We have a family dinner tonight, and those always last a long time. Could I come over this afternoon after my shift at the deli?"

Jessica thought about it. "We're usually off at about three thirty or four. If you want to come by the shop about then, we can walk to Sophie's house together."

"That's works for me." Tony started toward the counter.

Sophie added. "Come early and help at Great Finds."

He stopped at those words and turned back.

Sophie grinned. "Just kidding. See what happens when you tease me?"

Tony laughed. "I'll see you later."

14

A Way Out

When they finished their work for the day a little sooner than expected, Sophie and Jessica waited for Tony outside Great Finds. Sophie took a pad of paper and a pen out of her backpack. "Let's use this time and make a list of possible suspects."

"Everyone in the class, except maybe Emily."

Sophie wrote down the names. "And Mrs. Clayton. I don't want to put Uncle Sal on the list."

"No. I think he's honest. We don't know the names of the people who work there. Some of them seem kind of rough and tough."

"I noticed that too. I'll write 'workers.' We must be missing people because I don't see many real suspects on this list."

"That's true. We usually have suspicious people." Jessica bounced on her toes. "But I'm so glad I don't have to keep the secret from Tony this time. We've brought him into the mystery."

Sophie laughed. "Keep the secret?"

"I may have let a few facts slip in the past."

"A few?"

Jessica blushed. "More than a few, I admit. I'm not good with secrets. I try to be, but sometimes things slip out."

"I have to say that you've done well with everyone but Tony. This summer we've had some big secrets."

As Tony walked up to them, he said, "I have just over an hour before I have to be home."

They started toward Sophie's house at a brisk pace.

"Sophie, you don't have to run. Why don't you tell me about what I'm going to see."

She said, "If I described it, you'd think I'd dreamed it. We'll be there soon."

Jessica panted. "Sooner than usual." She gasped for air. "Can we slow down a little?"

Sophie eased off. But when they could see her house through the trees, she moved faster again.

Once inside, she grabbed the flashlight out of the kitchen drawer. With Tony and Jessica behind her, she hurried upstairs and into the guest room. Pointing at the closet, she said, "In there."

Tony leaned over to see inside the closet. "Winter coats?"

Sophie groaned. "Behind the coats. Here." She handed Tony the flashlight.

The sound of the flashlight turning on came only seconds before he said, "This can't be real!"

Sophie gestured toward the opening. "Let's go downstairs."

He stepped back out. "It's still a real staircase? The stairs go somewhere hidden?"

"That's what I wondered," Jessica answered. "When you see it, everything will make sense. Sort of. I'm still not sure why anyone would work in a basement."

Tony stepped into the closet and started down the stairs with the two girls close behind. At the bottom he paused. "Now I understand what you meant, Jessica. Did you find clues to whose office it was?"

"Mom gave us the clues we needed before we found it. The builder of this house lived here for a while."

"That makes sense. So those are house plans?" He pointed to the rolls of paper.

"Houses. Plus the boathouse."

He turned toward Sophie. "Seriously? Uncle Sal loves history. He's going be thrilled to have the original drawings for the factory."

When silence greeted him, he asked, "What aren't you telling me?"

"Let's show him the drawings, Jessica."

They went over to the table and first spread out the plans for Sophie's house and then for the factory. Shining the light on them, Sophie explained about the closet upstairs and the dashed lines. Then she opened the plans for the factory and showed him similar lines.

"You believe there's a secret passage in the Sweet Bites building?" He laughed. "I don't think that would have been missed all this time."

Sophie didn't say a word; she just gestured toward the stairs they'd come down.

When Tony looked that direction, he said, "You're right. You probably want me to ask Uncle Sal about trying to find this, don't you?"

"But we need to protect him and not say what we're searching for in case it's tied to the mystery. Our mysteries usually become dangerous."

"I know that's a fact." He paused. "I can ask to explore the building."

Sophie said, "I think we should do this when no one else is there."

"He goes to work very early, even on Saturday. He says he likes the quiet. Let's meet at six o'clock."

"Tonight?" Jessica asked with a hopeful tone in her voice.

"Tomorrow morning."

Jessica groaned.

Early Saturday morning, they got ready to go. After Jessica had showered, she stood in front of the mirror with her hair combed, but wet. Instead of drying and styling it, then putting on makeup, she pulled her hair back in a ponytail and turned toward the bedroom door. Sophie almost fell on the floor in shock.

Jessica only spoke one word after getting out of

bed: "Chocolate." Sophie had assumed that meant her cousin needed a piece of one of her favorite foods to help her wake up, so she'd gone to the kitchen to find the two small boxes of chocolates they'd been given and brought home. They'd eaten a piece out of each box the day before. Both now sat open and empty on the kitchen counter. Her mother wasn't kidding when she said she loved chocolate.

Sophie put some of Jessica's makeup in her cousin's purse. Once she was fully awake, she'd realize her mistake and might be upset. Then Sophie grabbed the page with the dashed lines on it from the roll of plans for the boathouse, folded it, and put it into her backpack. They walked to town in silence.

Tony was waiting in the open doorway of Sweet Bites with a paper sack in his hand when they arrived. "Good morning."

Jessica shook her head from side to side.

"Not a good morning? Is this Jessica every day?"

"Not every day. Mornings aren't her best time," Sophie explained. "Plus, this is the earliest we've had to get up this summer. I think she needs chocolate."

"I brought muffins from Bananas." He held up the bag. "Uncle Sal's back in his office. The door will lock when I close it." He opened the door wider so the girls could enter, then closed it behind them.

Once inside, Tony went straight toward the chocolate storage area, and they followed him. "Let's get Jessica a piece of chocolate and see if that revives her. We can all eat muffins after that."

In the room, Jessica took a deep breath. "I feel better already." She used tongs to take a piece of dark chocolate off a stack and popped it into her mouth. Pure happiness crossed her face. "If you give me a few minutes, I think I'll be fine."

Tony laughed. "You might need for your parents to buy a chocolate factory, Jessica."

"That's an amazingly great idea. I'll tell my mom and dad—when I finally get to see them again," she added with a sad voice.

Back in the entryway, Tony opened the bag of muffins and held it in front of Sophie. "I think I chose good ones for everyone."

"Mine must be the blueberry-banana muffin."

Jessica picked the chocolate chip–banana. "Very wise, Tony. Thank you."

"I now know you like chocolate." He reached into the bag and pulled out the last muffin. "I love Mrs. Bowman's banana-walnut." He crunched the bag into a ball and tossed it into the trash can.

Sophie finished her muffin first and brushed crumbs off her hands.

When Jessica finished her muffin, she seemed to be more herself. She touched her face and hair. "I forgot my makeup, and my hair is like yours, Sophie!"

"I can't help with your hair, but I put your makeup in your purse. What's wrong with my hair?"

"It's perfect on you. But it isn't me. Thanks for bringing my makeup."

Tony said, "You don't need it, you know. You're pretty without makeup."

Jessica smiled from ear to ear. "Thank you. Since you said that, I'll wait to put it on until we're done with our search. We have work to do."

Tony led them down the hall, took a turn at the end, went down another hallway, up steps to the left, and entered an office. "From the drawings, I think this could be the room."

Sophie tried to spread out the builder's drawing on a woman's desk, but it was too cluttered with papers and other things. She straightened up what she'd accidentally moved, then set the drawing on the floor and kneeled down to review it.

"I brought this because I thought it might give us clues. But studying it here, I'm realizing that all we know is that there are dotted lines on the left side of the building, toward the back, exactly where we are. The wall has been painted many times over the years. I wonder if it's been sealed over and the opening will be impossible to find."

"I'm surprised. You aren't usually so negative, Sophie," Tony said.

Sophie took a deep breath and gave the drawings another glance before speaking. "You're right. Let's find this," she said louder as she rose to her feet.

They checked along the wall, but it was smooth.

Tony said, "I have to agree with you on this one,

Sophie. If there used to be a secret passage on this wall, at some point it was painted or boarded over. Let's try another room." The three of them went out the door, down the hall, turned a corner, and turned another corner.

Jessica asked, "Where are you taking us, Tony?"

"I know from experience that all of these turns lead to an office right beside the one we were just in."

When they entered the room, they found three desks inside, but more importantly, decorative panels on all the walls. Sophie said, "This wall has secret panel potential."

"I think it's close to what it was when it was built. My uncle once showed a photo of this room to Nezzy Grant. You know old lady Grant."

Both girls nodded because they knew her very well.

"She remembered that this room was a place for the ladies to rest between dances when they had events here in the boathouse. She said it was very pretty and elegant with chandeliers and velvet chairs."

"It sure doesn't fit that description anymore. But the factory area itself has a little bit of old elegance left. I noticed pretty details on the ceiling. Things like that remind me of older buildings in some of the countries I've lived in."

"Maybe we'll find our secret passage here. I've spent time in this building to know that there's only one other room where it could be."

Each of them took a wall, and they began pushing and tapping.

After a while, Sophie thought she'd found something. "Jessica, listen to this." She rapped on her wall with her knuckles. "Doesn't this sound like it did in that closet?"

Jessica and Tony both hurried over. Sophie tapped along that edge, and then beside it. The sound was very different.

"You're right, Sophie! It's like the closet."

The three of them pushed on and tested the area around the spot with the hollow sound. Suddenly, the panel on the wall popped inward. Sophie grabbed the edge of the opening so she wouldn't fall.

"Who found it?" Sophie turned to Jessica and Tony.

"I think I did," Tony answered. "This area"—he tapped the corner of the rectangle—"moved when I pushed it."

"Good going, Tony." Sophie pushed the panel completely open.

Jessica leaned over to see into the passage. "It's like the other one."

"Except that we don't know where this one goes," Tony added.

Sophie pictured the boat dock with its new wood. "I think we do." She waited to see if Jessica or Tony thought the same thing.

Tony shrugged.

Jessica bounced on her feet. "I know! The dock with the boat! Nothing else makes sense."

"Yes. I don't know why, but the builder decided to create a way out of this room to the boat dock. Maybe he thought secret passages were fun."

Jessica nodded. "I know I do. I'd never seen one before I came to Pine Hill."

Sophie retrieved the flashlight from her backpack, turned it on, and shined it down in the hole.

Spiderwebs on the sides reflected back the light, and Jessica shuddered.

Tony noticed. "You don't like dark, unknown places?"

"That isn't it. I don't like spiderwebs. Sophie's secret staircase was full of webs."

Tony surprised Jessica by not laughing at her. Instead, he said, "I'll go get a broom out of the janitor's closet."

"Thank you, Tony. That's what we did at Sophie's house."

Tony left and was back in a few minutes. Then, broom in hand, he went ahead of them down the stairs, Sophie shining the light from behind him and Jessica following her.

"Don't worry, Jessica. Webs are on some of the side areas, but the passage itself is clean."

Jessica continued down the steps. "That's good and bad. I'm glad there aren't spiderwebs, but that shows us that someone's used this recently."

"Very recently," Tony added.

At the bottom of the circular stone staircase, there was a level area.

Sophie held the flashlight near her watch. "We've been at the factory awhile, so we'd better hurry. Our knowledge of this has to stay a secret. If we don't get out of here soon, someone who comes to work early may see what we're doing."

Tony moved faster. "Uncle Sal will be so surprised when he sees the staircase and this pathway!"

It felt to Jessica like they'd walked forever, but she knew they hadn't walked farther than the building was long. The brick path ended at a wooden wall.

Sophie said, "Step to the side, Tony. Let me shine the light on this wall so we can figure out how this opens because it must open."

"We know it opened a long time ago, but we don't know if it still does. What if someone found the opening, came down here, but couldn't find any way out?" Jessica said, "Or does Sophie the Detective say that it will open?"

"I still think that the rowboat out there in the boathouse is the same one that you and I saw on the lake, Jessica. It came from and returned this direction."

"Wait! There." Tony moved the flashlight in Sophie's hand back where it had just been. "This area with the small piece of wood on it appears worn, as if it's had more use than the rest of the boards." He pushed the small piece of wood to the side, but nothing happened. Sophie pushed it the other direction. Still nothing happened.

Jessica said, "Let me try. This must be the lever that opens it." Jessica stepped up and studied the piece of wood for a moment. "Sophie, shine the light in front of me. There are scratches that make a circle around here." When she had, Jessica reached up, took hold of the piece of wood, and slowly spun it. At the halfway mark, the door swung out. The boat dock lay in front of them and the rowboat beyond.

The three of them stared in silence.

Jessica spoke first. "The door is the wall under the stairs that had the cracked paint."

Sophie said, "Yes. They didn't use the stairs because they had this door."

Jessica turned to Sophie. "So you didn't need to climb them."

"Or fall through them," Tony added.

She rubbed her elbow and winced. "I sometimes wish I hadn't tried."

Jessica stepped outside and examined the lock. "I think I understand how this works. Close the door, and I'll try to open it."

Tony pushed it shut and waited. Scratching and scraping sounds made Sophie wonder if Jessica had really figured it out. Then the door creaked open.

"I did it. That didn't take long."

Sophie checked her watch and said, "No, but all of this took quite a while. Hurry. We need to get all the way up and out of this building before anyone arrives."

They raced back up the stairs and out through the

maze of hallways to the main entrance. The factory area was still silent, and all the lights were off in the offices they passed. They went out the door and sat down on the bench in front of the building. They hadn't been there long when Mrs. Clayton drove up to Sweet Bites and parked.

She got out of her car, gave them her usual smile, and said, "Good morning! You're here early. What's the special occasion?"

When Sophie was working on a mystery, she never gave out any extra information to people, in case they later became suspects. Keeping to her method, she simply said, "We wanted to be here early this morning." As Sophie entered the building, she realized that Mrs. Clayton was too nice to be part of their mystery. She should take her off their list of suspects.

15

The Second Suspect

Later that morning, Jessica looked up from the chocolate-making demonstration and saw a woman walk by. She seemed nervous, so Jessica asked Sophie, "Who's that?"

"Kelsey Newman," Sophie replied. "She grew up in Pine Hill, went away to college, and came home to take over her parents' flower shop, Buds & Blooms."

Jessica watched as the woman went down the hall and around the corner. It seemed odd that the owner of a flower shop would be in a chocolate factory, but it was a small town. Maybe she had a friend or someone in her family who worked here. But the way Kelsey had glanced over her shoulder as she walked, almost as if she wanted to see if anyone was watching her, made Jessica wonder if something was wrong.

Sophie must have thought the same thing because she whispered in Jessica's ear, "I'm going to follow her."

"I'm coming with you."

To not interrupt their class, Jessica whispered to Emily that they were going to the restroom. She could let Uncle Sal know if he asked. Then they walked away, heading down the hall in the direction Kelsey had gone. When they went around the corner, they found a hallway with closed doors. Continuing down the hallway, she heard raised voices through a closed door, so she and Sophie stopped.

A man's voice said, "Please help," then some other words she couldn't clearly hear.

A woman's voice said, "If I've told you once, I've told you ten times, a hundred times, Kirk, you've gotten yourself mixed up in something serious. Get out."

Sophie whispered, "I'm pretty sure that voice belongs to Kelsey. She has a younger brother named Kirk."

Kirk said several words that were too quiet for Jessica to understand. Then there were scraping sounds, like a chair sliding across the floor.

Sophie hurried down the hall with Jessica behind her. As Sophie pushed on the door to the women's restroom, the office door opened and Kelsey stepped out. The girls quickly darted into the restroom.

Inside the empty room, Jessica asked, "What do you think that was about?"

"It didn't sound good for Kirk."

A couple of minutes later, they went back in class.

While they'd been gone, the class had moved back to the enrober to make more chocolate-covered marshmallows. The good news was that it was milk chocolate again, so Sophie stood at the end and waited for the finished marshmallows to come out of the cooling section, eating one she was given with a smile on her face. Jessica might make a chocolate lover out of her yet.

They helped stack all of the new chocolates onto two trays. Uncle Sal gave Jessica one tray and old Mr. Pleckenpoll the other one. It seemed wise to break them up so one person couldn't trip and spill them all on the way to the chocolate storage room, but the old man had so much trouble walking that it appeared like he might fling his half of them on the floor any second. What happened the other day must have been a moment when he felt young. They delivered the trays with no incidents though.

After class, Sophie carefully took off her gloves and dropped them in the trash. Jessica did the same, but not until she'd licked the tip of one finger to get the chocolate off.

"Aren't you getting tired of chocolate yet?"

"I'm a little surprised, but I'm still having fun with it. On the flipside, are you enjoying chocolate more?"

Sophie turned to stare at the chocolate factory's floor. "Yes. I wouldn't mind having a piece or two of chocolate this weekend. I hope that Uncle Sal sends us home with some again."

As they walked toward the front of the building, Uncle Sal stopped them. "I understand that your mother loves chocolate, Sophie."

"I was surprised to find that out because she doesn't let us have dessert very often."

Jessica said, "She wants us to eat healthy."

Uncle Sal smiled widely. "Chocolate can be part of a healthy diet."

Jessica laughed. "I've always thought so."

"She does so much for our town that I'd like to do something for her. I've asked that a box of candy be left at the front desk for your mom. I hope she enjoys every bite. It's an assortment of milk and dark chocolate in different flavors."

"Thank you very much."

He walked on toward the factory floor, calling out to one of his workers, so Sophie and Jessica went on their way.

When they arrived at the front desk, no one was there. "Uncle Sal said that the box of candy would be here, but I don't see anything." Jessica stepped around the corner of the desk and turned in a full circle. "No, wait." A box of chocolates was pushed to the corner of the desk and had been wrapped in what they knew from their tour the first day was the factory's wrapping paper. Sophie joined her behind the desk.

"It was nice of him to wrap it for Mom." Sophie picked up the box.

"What if that box wasn't for her?"

"One box of chocolate would be the same as another. And he said it would be here at the front. We can wait a minute or two and see if anyone comes with another box, or if Mrs. Clayton returns. Maybe she went home early because it's Saturday."

Sophie sat down in Mrs. Clayton's chair and leaned back in it. "We've already followed Emily, so that leaves Dylan, his mother, and Mr. P. I doubt an old man is our thief. Dylan's mother talks all the time, and that wouldn't be a good quality for a thief, would it?"

They both laughed.

When Jessica turned toward the hallway, she saw someone moving away, another shadowy figure that shouldn't be there. No one had walked across the entry area from the factory or the hall, so this someone had been listening to them. This wouldn't be a good place to discuss the mystery.

Sophie leaned forward. "I probably shouldn't read something on Mrs. Clayton's desk, but this was sitting on top and caught my attention. It might be important. 'Erma, do you know if someone needed something from my desk? I noticed that things weren't the way I left them.' It's signed 'Shelley.'"

Sophie grimaced. "Jessica, I think there was a name sign on the desk I sat at with the factory's drawing this morning. I also think it said 'Shelley.' I'd like to get rid of this note, but that would make what happened even more suspicious if Shelley asked Erma about it later."

Jessica glanced over her shoulder to make sure no one was there. "I hope Erma and Shelley don't tell others. The criminals could start to wonder if someone's after them."

Sophie nodded. When two minutes had passed, Sophie stood, took the box of candy in her hands, and said, "I'd like to get out of here. This must be Mom's box."

Jessica shrugged. "Even if it isn't, they can easily make this box again for whoever was supposed to get it. It's on Mrs. Clayton's desk. If it's her box of chocolates, I don't think she'd mind. She always seems so happy and friendly. Let's go, Sophie."

When they stepped out the doors, no one was in sight except for a gardener working on the flowers in front of the building.

"That delay for the candy cost us time. I guess we're not learning anything more about a class member today," Jessica said. "But Soph, I saw another shadowy figure. I think someone was listening to us."

"It's hard to know who's a friend and who isn't in this mystery."

"I agree."

As they walked, Sophie said, "We might have to start watching the factory when everyone leaves for the day and follow one of them. If we find one who didn't drive to work, that is."

"Soph, I've been thinking about the secret passages. I know you don't like to tell people what we've learned until a mystery is solved, but you should tell your parents what we discovered."

Sophie was silent for a couple of minutes. "Let's keep it a secret for now. The staircase was hidden for a long time, so a few more days won't matter. The two hidden places are so much alike that the bad guys might pick up on a connection to us if Mom or Dad told people about it, and the story got back to them."

"That's a good point, Sophie. Who could resist telling everyone about a secret staircase?" When they could see the resort, Jessica looked up toward the roof. "I wonder if the helicopter is tied into this mystery at all."

"I don't know why it would be, Jessica. Tony's dad said it was a guest arriving. I know better than to ignore anything though. I guess it's possible."

Jessica said, "That day, when we were talking to people in the group of bystanders, I saw someone come out of the side door and go toward the back of the building, walking at a fast pace. He was wearing a suit and had on sunglasses. I thought he might be Agent Dallas of the F.B.I. I even asked the sheriff about him. And that's when she asked me to keep my eyes open at the factory."

Sophie stopped. "And you didn't think this was important to tell me?"

"We didn't have a mystery. All we had was a man in a helicopter."

Sophie groaned. "Are there any other clues that I should know about?"

"I don't think so."

"I would have investigated. His trail may have gone cold."

Jessica rolled her eyes. "You've been reading detective books again, haven't you?"

"Not my usual kind. This one's all about codes and spies. How spies hide things."

"And you're going to use that information how?"

"I may need to know how to write something in a code." Sophie gave Jessica a look that said she shouldn't argue with her.

"I never thought I would solve a mystery, so I won't say we'll never need a code."

Sophie gave a single nod. "Thank you. I like to have all the skills I can, so I'm ready for anything. I learned that the best code seems to be a simple one, at least it would be for our uses. A good one was used by someone almost two thousand years ago in Rome. All he did was move the letter down one, so if I wanted to write the letter *a*, I would use the letter *b*. If I wanted to write the letter *m*, I would use the letter *n*, and so on."

"That does sound fun. Are there any others?"

"See? I told you this was interesting. There are so many codes that it's hard for me to even remember them. But I'm working on it. The section about spies might be helpful in a mystery too. When a spy wants to leave something and let another spy know it's there so he or she can pick it up, they call it a 'dead drop.'"

Jessica shivered. "I don't like the word *dead* in there."

"I think they use that because it's not like you handed it to a living person. I've been thinking about places in Pine Hill that I could use for dead drops."

"Because there are so many times when you need to be a spy and hide something from another one?"

"You'll see. This will all come in handy. Maybe not on this mystery, but I'll need to know it sometime."

By now they had reached the edge of the parking lot. Sophie stared at the outside of the building for so long that Jessica wondered if they were going to start attracting attention.

"Soph, we need to move on."

"Maybe we should go inside and wait to see if that man comes through the lobby. You'd remember him, wouldn't you?"

"In a place where most people dress very simply and casually, a man in a suit would stand out. Of course, if he only wore the suit for his helicopter ride and then changed into jeans or something like that, I'm not sure I would recognize him."

Sophie started toward the resort's entrance. "Let's wait in the lobby. Mom's not expecting us for a while."

"But Sophie"—Jessica hurried after her—"what's our reason for being here? Two twelve-year-olds can't sit in a fancy resort's lobby for no reason at all." Jessica had caught up to Sophie, and they were almost to the doorman outside the resort.

Sophie checked the time on her watch. "I would ask if you wanted a milkshake—"

"With our chocolate samples, I've had too many sweets already today."

"I agree. But I remember hearing Mom tell Dad not too long ago that the resort is now serving 'light lunches.' I'm not sure what that means, but it's lunchtime, and I still have money left from my allowance. I wouldn't if Mom didn't keep giving us money for the deli."

"Then let's get lunch."

A "light lunch" turned out to be small things that cost a lot of money. So, instead of that, Sophie and Jessica each got a glass of iced tea, sat in the lobby, and waited.

Jessica glanced around at all the adults coming and going. "We're the only kids here. We can only stay here so long."

"Sip your tea slowly, and we'll go to Great Finds after this."

When they'd almost finished their drinks, they had to tell the waiter that they didn't want anything else when he came to check on them. Jessica said, "I think we're going to need to go soon, Sophie."

"I know." Sophie took a big drink from her tea and started to push it away.

Jessica noticed Mr. Pleckenpoll coming through the doors. "Sophie, there's Mr. P. Maybe we should go say hi to him on our way out." Jessica started to rise to her feet, but Sophie reached out and pushed down on her shoulder, and she sank back into her chair.

Sophie said, "That's Mr. P., all right, but are you noticing anything strange about him?"

"No." She watched him. "Wait! He's moving more quickly than we've seen him do before. In fact, he isn't moving like an old man."

"That's what I thought." When he stepped into an open elevator, Sophie stood. "Let's watch the numbers on the elevator and see what floor he gets off on."

The two of them hurried over to the elevator doors and watched the display until the elevator stopped.

Sophie said, "Five."

They hurried up the stairs that were beside the elevator, racing up toward the fifth floor. By the third floor, Jessica was panting. She felt like she'd climbed a mountain by the time they reached their destination.

Sophie pushed open the door to the fifth floor an inch or so. No one was in the hallway, so she opened it a bit more. Still nothing. Opening it all the way, she stepped out and peered around it.

Jessica whispered, "Anything?"

"No. The elevator moved a lot faster than we did. He's already in his room."

The carpeted hallway stretched before them in both directions. Hotel room doors lined the hallway on each side. A window at the end of the hall let in light, and the elevator sat at the other end. "Sophie, every door's closed."

Sophie started walking down the hall.

"Sophie, what are you doing? Someone might see us. And I don't think we're supposed to be here."

"We need to find out what room he's in."

"What are you proposing? That we knock on every door?" Jessica laughed.

"Not a bad idea."

"I was kidding! What reason could we give for knocking on doors?"

Sophie paused for a moment before speaking. "Maybe we can say we want to tell them about Mom's antique shop. While they're visiting, they could go there."

"Oh, right. Your mother would love that. And I'm saying that in a sarcastic way because she would hate it if we used her shop's name for this. And I don't think the hotel would appreciate it if someone from the town came in and started knocking on doors. It might get your mother in trouble with the resort."

Sophie's shoulders drooped. "You're right. It wasn't my best idea."

Jessica didn't say anything, but she had to agree.

"I guess we'll have to wait here until Mr. P. comes out of his room. Before you say it, I realize that's a bad idea too because someone might want to use the stairs and we can't explain why we're here."

A door halfway down the hall opened. Sophie jumped back into the stairwell, leaving the door open a crack. A man with dark hair peered out the door, looking first to the right and then to the left. Then he stepped out, closed the door, and hurried in their direction. Jessica hoped he was on his way to the elevators, not the stairs. She wanted to do a happy dance when he passed them. When he reached the elevator, he pushed a button, waited until the doors opened, and got on.

When the elevator doors closed, Jessica blew out a big breath. "That was close, Sophie."

"Tell me about it." Sophie turned and started descending the stairs. "We'd better hurry and get over to Great Finds so we can help Mom."

"And eat lunch!"

"That too."

"Let's follow Mr. P. after class on Monday and see if we can figure out his mystery."

"He seems like such a nice old man," Jessica said. "I hope he's not a bad guy."

When they arrived at the front of Great Finds, Sophie and Jessica peered in the window. Sophie said, "Mom is helping one person, and there are two—no, I see three other people waiting. I don't think we should bother her. She's going to be busy for a while. Let's go home and have something to eat there."

As they started toward home, she added, "And maybe we can have a piece of the chocolate in this box."

At Sophie's house, they made peanut butter and

jelly sandwiches and sat down to eat them at the kitchen table. After eating a peach for dessert, Sophie opened the wrapping paper on the box of chocolates. A computer-printed note was taped to the box. It read:

Please make sure these end up with the right person.

16

Sparkling Surprise

"Sophie, this box of candy might not have been for your mother," Jessica said as she stared at the note.

"You may be right, but we've already opened it, and if it's a gift for someone, we've ruined it. Maybe we should call the factory and ask Uncle Sal about it."

Jessica nodded. "Very good idea."

Sophie looked up the phone number and dialed the chocolate factory. After five rings she hung up. "Mrs. Clayton must have left for the day, and no one else is answering. We can't return it today. Uncle Sal promised Mom a box of candy, and we have one right here."

"I guess we may as well eat what's inside. He can make a new box for the other person on Monday," Jessica said

Sophie lifted the lid. "Twelve pieces of candy, half dark chocolate and half milk chocolate. I've decided that I like milk chocolate more." Sophie reached for a piece of the lighter brown candy.

"I'm for dark chocolate all the way." Jessica reached for the darker chocolate. "Now the question is, what flavor is it?" Jessica took a little nibble off a corner. Then a slightly larger nibble. "I think this one is orange-filled."

Sophie broke hers in half.

"I wish you wouldn't do that. It makes a pretty piece of chocolate ugly."

Sophie laughed. "And a bite out of the corner doesn't?"

Jessica stared at the piece of chocolate in front of her. "I suppose you're right."

Sophie poked at the filling oozing out of one of her chocolate halves. "It's caramel, I think. You're the chocolate expert. It shouldn't have a red center, should it?"

"Only if Uncle Sal is trying one of his strange combinations again. Caramel and jelly filling is weird." Jessica leaned over to see it.

Sophie stared at the jelly-filled center. "Jessica"—she reached into the gooey center and pulled out something hard—"this isn't jelly." She rolled the hard candy center in her fingers and held it up. A red stone, something that would be in a ring or a necklace, caught the light coming through the kitchen window.

She looked up in time to see Jessica about to take a bigger bite of her piece of chocolate. She shoved her cousin's hand away from her mouth. "Don't eat that!"

Jessica rubbed the spot on her hand where Sophie had pushed her. "Ouch. Why did you do that?"

She held the stone where Jessica could see it. "I'm guessing, but aren't rubies red?"

"Yes! What have we gotten in the middle of this time?" Jessica picked up the piece of chocolate that had been knocked out of her hand and had fallen to the floor. She pulled it in half. "This one only has a normal filling in it. Jewels inside chocolates are a good reason for criminals to be in Pine Hill. I would think that a real ruby this size—if that's what it is—would be worth a lot of money."

Sophie reached for another piece of chocolate, but Jessica put her hand on Sophie's. "Maybe we should leave these all alone."

"I want to see what's in the rest of them, and we already have two of them open."

Jessica stared at the box for so long that Sophie wondered what she was going to do or say. When her cousin reached for a piece of milk chocolate, Sophie knew that Jessica had decided to break them open.

A minute later, a dozen pieces of chocolate, now in half, sat in front of them on the table.

"Only your first piece had the gemstone in it, Sophie. If it is a ruby, it's worth a lot of money."

"It must be real. Why would someone hide a fake gemstone inside a piece of chocolate?"

"Maybe as a surprise for someone?" Jessica said.

"It sure would be a surprise if someone bit into a piece of chocolate and had their teeth hit something hard. I don't think that would be a good idea. If their teeth didn't hit it, they might choke on it. That's a bad idea all around."

"You're right. But if that's the case, then we have somehow stumbled upon some major criminals. Because I have a feeling that this gemstone is worth more money than even you and I can imagine."

Sophie stood. "Let's rinse it off so we can see better what we found." She went across the kitchen, opened the cupboard, and pulled out a fine mesh strainer. "My mom uses this to drain the juice off canned pineapple and other stuff. We won't lose the stone down the drain if we put it in here."

"Great idea."

At the sink, Sophie ran hot water through the strainer. "I want to make sure it doesn't wash away by accident." She removed the gem from the strainer and patted it dry with a kitchen towel. Then she held it up to the sunlight, and it sparkled even more than before.

"That's beautiful! I remember when we went to see the crown jewels in London. They're the jewelry from kings and queens. This is pretty enough to be in a crown. We have to take it to Sheriff Valeska."

"I won't argue with you this time, Jessica. We do need to get this to the sheriff as fast as we can."

She took out a small plastic zipper bag from a

drawer and slipped the stone inside. While she did that, Jessica picked up the pieces of chocolate and the box and put them in a larger plastic bag that Sophie stowed in her backpack. With the zipper bag tucked in Sophie's front jeans pocket and the backpack over her shoulders, they went out the door, down the steps, and started on the trail through the woods toward town.

Every once in awhile, Sophie patted that pocket with her right hand. Finally, Jessica asked, "Are you worried you're going to lose it?"

"Yes! I don't want to have to search through the woods to find one red stone. I put it in my pocket because that felt safer." Sophie chewed on her lip. "Jessica, I keep feeling like Sheriff Valeska is going to be upset with us because we have the gemstone, but—"

"Sophie, it isn't our fault. Uncle Sal promised you a box of chocolates. We picked up a box of chocolates. End of story."

"Then let's think about the next step in solving this mystery."

"I don't know if we have a next step, Sophie. The sheriff will say to stay out of it now."

"No, we're inside the chocolate factory. She may need us to keep our eyes open or do something else. She knew something was going on, or she wouldn't have asked you to spy."

"That's what keeps going through my head. But she said it wouldn't be dangerous. Even when she told me to stop watching, she said it wasn't dangerous."

The two of them walked a couple of minutes without saying anything. Then Sophie stopped right in the middle of the trail and turned to Jessica, who barely managed to stop before running into Sophie's back. "We still don't know what's going on. Why would she ask you to spy for her if it didn't matter?"

Jessica tugged on Sophie's arm, and they started moving forward again on the trail. "Maybe we'll get some answers today. I don't think Sheriff Valeska was expecting us to find a box of chocolates with a gemstone in it."

Sophie stopped again, and this time Jessica did ram into her back.

"Sophie! Stop doing that."

"Sorry. I wondered again if this is a real stone. If it's fake and someone put it in the candy . . ." Sophie shook her head. "That doesn't make any more sense now. Why would anyone hide fake gemstones?" Sophie started on her way again, and Jessica stepped beside her as the path widened nearer to town so she wouldn't hit Sophie if she stopped.

They continued walking and soon could see the town in front of them. Continuing down the sidewalk, they quickly arrived at the sheriff's office. Sophie pushed the door open and entered with Jessica behind her. Sheriff Valeska sat at her desk, working on her computer.

The sheriff looked up, spotted them, and said, "Oh no. What now, Sophie?"

Sophie glanced over her shoulder at the secretary, Clare Morton. She still didn't feel comfortable speaking in front of her. And one of the deputies was working in the back at a filing cabinet. "Sheriff, we have something to show you, but it's kind of a secret. Could we step into one of those rooms?" Sophie gestured with her head toward the room they'd been in the other day.

Sheriff Valeska pushed back from her desk and stood. "Today is busy, so I hope it's important." The sheriff waved her hand at the room's open door. Sophie and Jessica walked in, the sheriff came in behind them and left the door partly open. "What is it, Sophie?"

Sophie glanced around them to make sure no one else was there. Then she reached into her pocket, pulled out the zipper bag with the ruby, and handed it to the sheriff.

Sheriff Valeska stared at the bag, her eyes growing wider and wider as she realized what was inside it. In a serious tone of voice, she slowly said, "Sophie, Jessica, where did you find this?"

17

Danger!

Chills went down Jessica's spine. She quickly explained to the sheriff about the box of chocolates Uncle Sal had promised them and how Sophie had found the stone in one of the chocolates in the box they'd picked up from the receptionist's desk.

Sophie pulled the pieces and box out of her backpack and handed the bag to Sheriff Valeska. "Do you have any idea why the ruby was in here?"

The sheriff slowly shook her head from side to side, then suddenly nodded up and down as if she'd realized something. "There's a man here in town who I believe can tell us more about this. I thought he was mistaken about what he expected to find in Pine Hill, what he trailed to this area. But"—she rolled her finger over the gemstone, flipping it around in her hand—"I think you've proven his theory to be correct."

She slowly raised her gaze from the ruby and looked at the two of them. "Will anyone suspect one of you when this box of chocolates comes up missing?"

Sophie and Jessica looked at each other, and Jessica said, "Oh no."

Sheriff Valeska said, "I take that as a yes."

Jessica said, "Yes. It's a definite yes. As we told you, Uncle Sal said there would be a box of chocolates sitting there. It was the end of the day, so maybe no one has tried to find them yet."

Sheriff Valeska glanced from one girl to the other and paused, seeming to mull something over. "I'm going to let the two of you in on a secret—"

"Is this more about why you asked me to watch things at the factory?"

The sheriff said, "No, Jessica. That was completely because of the recipe. I felt that Sal Donadio's factory was the least likely place to have danger, and that's the only reason I asked you to watch. Let me go make a phone call. I'll be right back." The sheriff left the room and closed the door behind her.

"What have we accidentally gotten ourselves into, Sophie?"

"I'm not sure, Jessica, but it sounds like it could be something dangerous. Maybe the most dangerous thing we've been in the middle of yet."

"I wish you hadn't said that. We've had so many things happen this summer, scary things, that I don't want this one to be any worse. I don't want there to be another mystery at all."

The sheriff came into the room a few minutes

later. "I spoke with that person and learned more. He thinks there's a criminal band working in this area, people who are involved with a gemstone theft ring. He hoped to contact me to make an arrest soon at the chocolate factory because he's become suspicious about things going on there and has been watching the front of the building every night."

"That means that he'll see someone leaving the candy factory with . . ."

The sheriff nodded. "Right, Sophie. With nothing. The box of candy with the ruby inside is gone. I can't stop anyone. I can't arrest anyone. I can't do anything. Someone in this ring must work there, at least one of them must."

"Remember, Sophie, that Uncle Sal says that people who work there can take home chocolate every day. No one would notice if someone had the chocolates. They could normally walk out the front door with them. It should be easy for Uncle Sal to make a new box like this."

"But, Jessica, I think it's pretty likely that someone is going to find out quickly that the gemstone isn't in the box of chocolates they got from the factory. Even if we find a way to leave a new box there, it won't help."

"Yes. And if they're smart, and they probably are, they may already know that someone is watching the front."

Sophie gulped. "And they'll also figure out or at least suspect that Jessica and I have their special box of chocolates. No matter how you look at it, we have a problem."

Jessica said, "But we could go inside the chocolate factory, sneak in, make a new box of chocolates, and put it where this one was."

Sophie nodded. "We picked up this box at the very end of the day, and Mrs. Clayton had already left early, so—"

Jessica jumped in, "So we might be able to get this back on her desk before anyone knows it's missing."

"Girls, I can't let you do that. If you walk in the front door of the candy factory, a hundred people might see you doing that. Even if we ask Sal Donadio to let you in that door on Sunday, people could be nearby and see you. I can't risk your being exposed."

"But, Sheriff, almost anyone would figure out that we have the box of chocolates. Uncle Sal said it was out front, and there were a lot of people around then. Besides"—Sophie grinned—"we don't have to walk in the front door."

"No, we have a better way."

"This I have to hear. The only other entrance into the place is the emergency escape to the roof, which leads to a ladder down the back of the building."

The idea was interesting. "We didn't know about that."

The sheriff said, "But you could still have someone see you on top of the roof. No, I have to protect you girls. You're my responsibility."

Jessica pretended to swim, swinging her arms in the air as though she was cutting through water.

"Swim? There's no way in from the lake. I know that to be a fact."

"Sheriff, I don't know who started that rumor, but it isn't true."

"And you know that because . . .?

Expecting Sheriff Valeska to be none too happy about their earlier trip to the factory, Jessica clenched her teeth.

"We swam there"—Sophie held up one hand when she saw the sheriff about to reprimand her—"with Mr. Donadio giving permission first, and Tony going with us so there was a family member. After I saw the boats on the lake, I wanted to see if there was a boat under the factory."

"And? Was there a boat under the factory?"

"An old rowboat, but we couldn't tell if it had been used."

Jessica said, "But we found a secret passage! We can go from it into the factory."

The sheriff laughed. "I haven't seen that, and I've been in that factory many times."

Jessica nodded. "It's there."

Sheriff Valeska sighed. "I guess we could send a boat to take you underneath the boathouse."

"No, Sheriff! That won't work because people could see it and hear the motor. If we swim tomorrow, it's Sunday, when the factory is closed for the day. No one will know we're there."

"I'm hesitant to tell Sal Donadio that you're doing this because I'm not sure who he trusts and who he might tell. It's private property though—"

"The last time we went, he told Tony that if we wanted to go under there and swim around and have fun, it was no matter to him."

"Then set this up with Tony, and let's do this. I don't see any other way to make it happen." After another hesitation, the sheriff added, "Girls, I need for you to stay away from my office for a while. You're at the chocolate factory almost every day, and people in Pine Hill know that you've solved two mysteries. If they see you coming in and out of here often, they may start to think that you're involved in a mystery again."

Sophie said, "But Sheriff, what if we find an important clue?"

The sheriff sighed. "Let's hope that doesn't happen, Sophie. I don't even want you to call here or for Jessica to send a text message with her phone. I don't have a better solution."

"I do! I read about it in one of my books. It's called a dead drop, a place where we can leave things for each other, but no one else will know they're there."

The sheriff laughed. "Sophie, that sounds like something out of a spy movie. This is Pine Hill."

"But, Sheriff, it would work."

"So where do you suggest we have this dead drop?"

Sophie's mind raced. They needed a place that would be easy to get to but where no one else would think to look. Her favorite bench in town came to mind, the one she always sat on when she wanted to figure things out. "The bench on the sidewalk over by Bananas Bakery. If something were taped underneath it, no one would know it was there."

"I can live with that, Sophie."

"We'll make a chalk mark on the side of the bench's armrest to let you know when there's something for you to pick up."

Sophie thought over the chalk that was in a box of toys from when she was little. "A line made from bright blue chalk."

"That won't be obvious, will it?" Jessica said sarcastically.

"Okay, white chalk. That might look more like dust, so it won't stand out as much."

The sheriff agreed.

"And when you've picked it up, Sheriff, wipe off the chalk mark so we know it's been done. We also need a code so no one else will be able to read the note."

Sheriff Valeska groaned. "Okay. What's the code?"

"I've read about so many good ones." She turned to Jessica. "Let's use the one I told you about earlier." When Jessica nodded, Sophie described it to the sheriff.

Ten minutes later, Sophie left the sheriff's office,

and she marched importantly down the street with her cousin. Sheriff Valeska had put her in charge of what they would do tomorrow afternoon. Well, her, Jessica, and Tony in charge. Her footsteps slowed as she realized that this could land them in the middle of danger.

Jessica said, "Sophie, why are we stopped here?"

Sophie noticed that she was standing in front of Buds & Blooms. "I just realized that we were going into a place tomorrow where someone works who either stole very expensive gemstones or helped someone who did."

"And you just thought of this? I thought of it from the first second that you suggested the idea. But I don't know of any other way to make this work." When a family walked by, she realized they were far from alone here. "There are quite a few people here. Maybe we should head toward home and talk about it there."

"You're right." Sophie gave a glance toward Buds & Blooms. When the owner looked up, Sophie gave a small wave. "I might buy Mom a flower sometime soon. She'd like that."

"Do you think the owner of this business has any connection with the gemstones?"

"I'm not sure of anything anymore. You were a spy who was supposed to find a spy, or at least watch out for one, but now we have a major criminal—or more than one—working in the chocolate factory. I hope that Uncle Sal is wrong about someone stealing his recipes though, because one crime is more than enough."

"Being a secret spy was kind of fun for a little while. But I'm glad we're working on this together now, Sophie."

18

More Chocolate

When the girls got back to Sophie's house, they went into the kitchen for a snack. Sophie grabbed a bag of trail mix—a mixture of nuts and dried fruit—out of the cupboard. When she went over to the refrigerator to get juice for them, she stopped and stared at the door.

Jessica took a handful of the trail mix. "Anything wrong?"

Sophie removed a note from the fridge. "We didn't have anything cold for our lunch, so I didn't see this note. Dad is reminding me that we're going to dinner tonight. But I don't remember—"

"Isn't it your mom's birthday today?"

"Oh no! I've been thinking about our mystery, and I didn't think about Mom. That isn't good."

"I've been with you almost all the time, so my guess is that you haven't gotten her a birthday gift or a card, right?"

"Very right. Dad must have left the note for me

this morning. We need to hurry back to town so I can find something."

"Maybe you'll see a store and think of a gift you could buy there that your mom would like."

"Mom has so many things because of the store she owns. Her store's where other people want to buy their gifts."

They each ate a handful of trail mix and drank a glass of juice before going to town on their usual path through the woods. Sophie didn't find anything on Main Street that felt like a good gift for her mom. They turned onto another street and came to a corner. She hadn't noticed earlier that the Down Shoppe, an important place in another mystery, was gone and the fishing store, Hook, Line & Sinker, was back there where it should be. Buds & Blooms was across the street.

After crossing the street, Sophie paused at the flower shop's window. "I talked about getting Mom a flower to make her happy, but a whole bunch of flowers might make her very happy. Maybe this is a good birthday present for her. She doesn't buy flowers for herself, other than the ones she plants at our house that she has me weed."

Sophie pulled open the door to the shop and walked inside with Jessica right behind her. Kelsey was helping someone at the counter, so Sophie and Jessica wandered around and looked at the bouquets. There were price tags on a few of them. Sophie leaned over to see one and groaned. "Jessica, I don't think I can afford to get Mom flowers with what Dad gave me for her birthday." She held up the tag for Jessica to see, and her cousin grimaced.

"You may be right. But before we go, let's ask and make sure. Maybe these bouquets are more expensive because of the kind of flowers or something like that."

Sophie chewed on her lip a second, staring at the vases filled with flowers. She still wasn't sure if she should leave or if she should ask. But she could hear her dad's voice telling her, "There's no such thing as a stupid question." When the other customer exited, Kelsey came over. "Can I help you, Sophie?"

Sophie hesitated for a second. "I'm not sure, Kelsey. My mom's birthday is today—"

"And you came here to buy her a gift! That's wonderful. I'm sure I can help you."

"I don't know, Kelsey. This is how much money Dad gave me to buy a gift." Sophie set the money on the counter.

"Are some flowers less expensive than others?" Jessica asked.

"Absolutely. I can make you a beautiful bouquet of flowers, Sophie. Do you need them to be in a vase?"

"Mom has a lot of pretty vases in her store."

Kelsey laughed. "That's partly why the flower bouquets near the entrance are so expensive. They're in antique vases from your mom's shop. Give me about ten minutes, and you can take your flowers with you." Kelsey went into a glass-fronted refrigerator filled with buckets of flowers.

Sophie felt stress ooze out of her. She would have a gift for her mom.

As they walked around the store, waiting for the flower arrangement, something caught Sophie's eye. "Jessica," she said in a low voice, "there are chocolates here."

"I know that lots of times people buy chocolates and flowers together as a gift. My dad has done that for my mom before."

"These aren't just any chocolates. These are from Sweet Bites Chocolates."

Jessica stepped closer. "Sophie, the chocolates are made in this town, so that isn't a surprise."

"But no one else sells them. At least not that I know of, which is strange."

Kelsey stepped out with a pretty bouquet of what Sophie recognized as daisies and carnations, along with other things she couldn't put a name to. She knew her mother would love it because it had an old-fashioned look that reminded her of the things her mother sold in her store. It wasn't too modern.

Kelsey said, "I see you noticed the chocolates that I have there. I'm the only store in Pine Hill that sells them. For some reason the factory wants them to ship to other places and not be sold here." She paused and seemed almost nervous when she added, "My brother Kirk talked me into carrying them here in the store and managed to talk Sal into letting me do it." Then the shadow lifted, and she smiled brightly again, maybe too brightly.

Sophie paid for the flowers Kelsey had wrapped with green paper. Then they went out the door. Standing outside, Sophie said, "Don't you think it's strange that only one store can sell Sweet Bites Chocolates?"

"I think people who visit Pine Hill would love to buy some. It doesn't make sense to me. Do you think it's another clue?"

Sophie turned and studied the building they'd left. "Maybe we should set up surveillance and watch to see who comes and goes."

"Who would we be watching for? People who like chocolate? Or flowers? I don't see how we would learn anything."

"I guess you're right. But something doesn't feel right about this place." Sophie began walking again, and Jessica stepped beside her.

"This time, I agree with you. But we'll have to see if any other clues lead back to Buds & Blooms. Well, any clues other than the owner and her brother having an argument."

Neither of them said anything for a while. Finally, as the shortcut to Sophie's house came into view. Sophie said, "Let's get ready for dinner. Tomorrow we have church. Then adventure."

The next morning, Sophie dressed in tan pants and a forest green T-shirt slid into the pew next to

Jessica who wore a light pink dress with white sandals. It was Sophie's usual look, but a little dressier for church. She'd worn a dress for dinner last night and didn't want to wear one again today. Jessica loved dressing up for church and everywhere else she could. She'd worn a dress last night too.

Sophie leaned over to her. "I've been thinking about swimming today."

Jessica raised one eyebrow.

Maybe they shouldn't talk about that here. Sophie glanced past Jessica and over to the opposite side of the church. "Dylan and his mother are over there. They're on our unknown list."

Jessica twisted in her seat so she could see the pair. The college student from their class was next to his mother, and she was talking—at least Sophie figured she was talking since her lips were moving.

In a low voice Sophie said, "I'm surprised she doesn't run out of breath. If I blow up a couple of balloons, I start to hurt inside. And she must blow out that amount of air as she speaks."

Jessica agreed. "It is amazing to see. And hear."

"You girls shouldn't speak about anyone that way," Mrs. Sandoval said from beside Sophie.

"Sorry, Mom. Mrs. Hanley seems like a good person. But it's hard to get in a word when she's nearby."

"Still, Sophie. Be kinder. I don't know someone with that name. Who are you talking about?"

Sophie turned again toward the mother and son.

"Dylan and his mother are in our chocolate-making class."

"Ah, yes. She came in the store one day this week. It was an afternoon, so it must have been after your class. Very nice woman. Kind. But I have to agree with you. I believe she said more words in the twenty minutes she was in the store than most people say in hours. I asked where she was visiting from. She told me all the places she had lived in her life, and it seems like they moved around a lot when she was young." Mrs. Sandoval smiled.

"I think her son is a little stressed-out."

"Where are you and Jessica going swimming today? I heard you ask her about it."

Sophie gave her best smile but knew it probably didn't look real. "In the lake. Over by the chocolate factory, I think. We're meeting Tony."

To her relief, the minister walked to the front of the church and up to the pulpit. Sophie knew not to say anything to Jessica during the rest of the service and worked to push the mystery out of her mind for the next hour. Even though they had excitement coming later today.

19

Chocolate-Covered Clue

Jessica swam up to the dock where Tony and Sophie already sat waiting. She leaned her elbows on it and looked up at them. "Sophie, you normally plan things very well, so well that we both have plastic bags with things we need taped to our backs including the tape to put them back on for our swim out. But we may have forgotten something."

Sophie stood. "We're here, and no one spotted us yet. I think everything's okay."

Jessica climbed the ladder and stood beside Sophie as Tony rose to his feet. "There's just one thing. We're dripping wet, so we're going to leave a trail of water down the hall."

Sophie put her hand over her mouth and groaned. "You are so right. We know where the bathroom is, so let's go inside the building, run in there to get the paper towels, and dry off. After that, we'll quickly wipe up the floor. That way if there's a security guard, he or she won't spot it."

"That sounds like a plan. It's about the only thing we can do if we want to get this job done today."

"There's one other thing, Tony. Jessica and I know how the chocolates are made because we've been in the class this week, so we're the best chance we've got for fixing this. We'll take the lead on the project."

Tony said, "I'd rather be in the middle of it all, but I see your point. The only thing I know about chocolate is how to eat it."

Jessica peeled the bags off Sophie, and Sophie did the same for her. After Sophie had taken a flashlight out of one, Jessica opened the door slowly.

Sophie whispered, "It wouldn't be good if someone came out this way right now."

When they were sure the passage was empty, Sophie led the way with the flashlight through the passage and up the stairs. Tony pushed the lever, and the panel into the office area opened. Sophie switched off the flashlight and left it on the top stair.

After stepping from the opening into the room, they hurried over to the door, and Sophie slowly opened it. She whispered, "All clear."

Tony whispered back, "We have to hurry. I couldn't figure out a good way to ask if there would be a security guard here today. If there is one, we don't know if that person is going to be passing this way any second."

All three of them jumped when they heard what

sounded like something falling off a desk or a shelf from somewhere in the building. They froze in place.

After a minute with no sounds, Sophie whispered, "Dry off in the restroom first. Then meet in the chocolate storage area. Since they keep some of the chocolate boxes and the papers that go around each piece there, along with the chocolates, we'll have everything we need."

Jessica and Tony nodded, then hurried down the hall. Jessica didn't even break the silence in the restroom. She kept thinking about how easily they could be caught.

Sophie whispered, "We dried off so much in the passageway that I don't think we dripped anywhere."

Jessica nodded agreement. She and Sophie hurried down the hallway, past Mrs. Clayton's desk, and into the factory. They found Tony pacing back and forth in the chocolate storage room.

Sophie took charge. "Jessica, you find all of the chocolates. Tony, you and I will stand guard. Then Jessica and I can put the box of chocolates together."

Sophie was always very organized at times like these. Jessica didn't like it when the door closed and she was alone in here, but having two guards was better than one.

She pulled her phone out of the plastic bag she'd had taped to her back and compared the photos of the chocolates that they'd taken with the pieces on the shelves, choosing those they needed and putting them in paper wrappers in the same size box as the one they'd taken home. She found the first few pieces quickly. It took a little longer to find the others because there were so many that were similar.

Jessica soon knew she'd chosen the exact right chocolates and only needed the final piece. It was the most important one, though, because it would have the ruby inside. Even though there were neat stacks of the many kinds of chocolate with no empty spaces, that piece of chocolate wasn't here. It had been milk chocolate with caramel in the middle and white chocolate lines on top.

Sophie walked in the door, startling Jessica, who clamped her own hand over her mouth so she wouldn't scream. When she saw it was her cousin, she pulled her hand away. "Sophie, don't scare me like that."

"What's taking so long? We need to get out of here as soon as we can."

She pointed at her phone. "I don't see this one." Jessica gestured at the shelves. "Help me find it."

Sophie looked at the phone, then went through the pieces on the shelf. "You're right. I don't see it either."

A voice from behind them said, "What's taking so long?"

Both Sophie and Jessica jumped and squealed.

"Tony Donadio, you are lucky that the door is closed or someone might have heard us." Sophie shook her head.

Jessica gestured to a shelf stacked with chocolates. "Tony, the piece that had the ruby in it doesn't seem to be here. But the milk chocolate with caramel inside looks like it, except it doesn't have white chocolate lines across the top."

"We can add white chocolate to the plain piece," Sophie suggested.

"Sophie, we don't know how to do that."

"I helped Mom decorate a cake once. It looks like it should be pretty simple. But maybe you should grab a few of those pieces of chocolate in case I don't get it right the first time."

Jessica put three onto a paper towel from a roll in there. "Good idea."

"I help decorate some foods at the deli when we're getting ready for parties, and this doesn't look too much different, so I can try too."

Jessica added one more piece of chocolate to the pile in her hand.

"Okay, let's finish this up."

Tony peered out the room's door, waved them on, and they hurried down to the factory, where they found a couple of glass containers and filled them with some of the warm, melted milk chocolate and white chocolate. Using a small knife, Jessica made a slit in the bottom of one piece of candy. Then Sophie opened a second plastic bag and brought out the ruby. Jessica pushed it inside the slit.

"You know, I don't think anyone's going to be able to tell we did this once we've put a little bit of milk chocolate on the bottom. I think this is going to look perfect. We do need for it to dry quickly though."

After Sophie put a small blob of milk chocolate on a piece of plastic, Jessica gently set the piece of chocolate with the ruby inside on top.

Sophie said, "I think if we dip a fork into the white chocolate, we can drizzle it across. It won't be as good as the equipment they've got here, but it will be a lot easier to clean up. Should I go first, Tony?"

Tony said, "If you think you can do it, go ahead. I've never said I was an artist. "

Sophie dipped the ends of the fork into the white chocolate, lifted it, and let some of it drip off. Following the pattern on the photo on Jessica's phone, she swung the fork over the piece of chocolate twice to give it the white chocolate zigzag on top. The first line went perfectly—and then a giant blob fell off the fork.

Sophie groaned. "Let's get the ruby out of here and into another piece of chocolate."

"We should have waited to fix the bottom of the piece of chocolate until we knew we had the top right."

"But then we might mess up the chocolate on top and have to fix the bottom. No, I think we did it in the right order. We have to start over."

Jessica said, "Tony, you get the ruby out of the piece of chocolate, and I'll make a slit in the bottom of another piece."

When that had been done, they sealed the bottom as they had before with new milk chocolate. Then Sophie handed the fork to Tony.

He dipped it into the white chocolate and drizzled it across the chocolate piece and back. All three of them studied the piece of chocolate from different angles. Jessica held her phone up next to it so they could all see it. "What do you think? Is it the same? I mean, exactly the same?"

"Almost," Sophie said. "The one in the picture seems to start on one corner and end on another corner. Tony's version isn't quite on the corner."

"Do you think we have to be that exact?" Tony asked.

Sophie nodded. "When your uncle explained the pieces of chocolate and how you could tell one from another by the pattern on the outside, he said it was important that each be *exactly* the same. That's the word he used. We'd better try one more time." She looked up at the clock. "We've already been here an hour. I hate to try again in case it's a complete disaster. But I think we better."

They did everything as before. When it was time for the white chocolate, Tony asked, "Who should do this one?"

Sophie patted Tony on the shoulder. "You got it way closer than I did, so I say we have you do it."

Tony gave a single nod, and then he went to work. The first line was perfect, but his hand shook, and Jessica could see he was about to freeze up before he swung the fork back to finish it. "You can do it, Tony!" Jessica said.

"Yes, you can," Sophie agreed.

Tony drizzled the white chocolate across the piece, ending in the corner and lifting the fork away so it couldn't drip down the side.

This time when they compared it to the original in the photo, it was the same.

"All right, Tony! Now we need for this to dry somehow, fast. Then put this in the box, wrap it, and get out of here."

Jessica motioned toward the office half of the building. "We passed what I think was a place for workers to have lunch. The chocolate should harden up quickly if we put the piece in the refrigerator in there."

Sophie picked up the plate with the piece of chocolate on it and carefully carried it in that direction.

"While you're gone, I'm going to clean up here so no one will think anything's wrong if they happen to come by."

"I'll help her," Tony said

Jessica set the last piece of the original chocolates on some plastic and crumpled up the paper towel that had somehow gotten a smear of white chocolate on it. "I would normally eat these messed up pieces to get rid of the evidence, but I'm too nervous to eat anything."

The nearby trash can was empty. "The janitor

must have already come, so anything we throw in there will stand out. Tony, I do think we have to eat the chocolate. It's one for each of us, and then we can put the piece we didn't need back in the storage room. It's still perfect."

Jessica popped the candy in her mouth. Her taste buds decided that it was a good time to eat chocolate after all, proving that there was no bad time for chocolate.

She'd have to tell her mother that the next time she saw her, but she couldn't let her know what she'd been doing when she'd figured that out because it might scare her. Being on the other side of the world and having her daughter get into all of these mysteries must have been hard for her. It had been hard for Jessica not to have her nearby when everything had happened with their mysteries this summer.

Tony wiped down their work area. Jessica could tell he was used to cleaning at the deli. The counter and sink sparkled, and the floor was clean. Jessica held on to the paper towel. She'd have to take it back with her. Or maybe she could hide it somewhere in the factory where she could find it the next day and throw it away. Trash didn't mean anything when there was more of it in the trash can.

Footsteps sounded in the hallway. Heart racing, Jessica turned to Tony. She swallowed hard, then whispered, "Sophie wouldn't make that much noise. What do we do?"

The two of them glanced around. Mr. Donadio's big old desk in the corner of the room was the only piece of furniture that wasn't completely open underneath. She tugged on Tony's sleeve, and they both hurried over to it and slid underneath, their knees up near their chins.

Someone entered the room and stopped.

Jessica pictured the place they'd just left. The piece of chocolate they hadn't altered was still sitting out.

The person walked around the room and then got farther and farther away, so he or she must have gone down the hall.

The two of them crawled out from under the desk and peered over the top of it. No one was there. When they stood, Jessica saw that the piece of chocolate was gone. She looked at Tony and back down at the place where the chocolate had been.

He grabbed her by the arm, and they hurried down the hall to the lunchroom where they stepped inside and found Sophie with a scared expression on her face.

Tony said, "You'll—"

Jessica shook her head. Telling Sophie now would only make her more nervous. She and Tony were nervous enough for the group.

He seemed to understand what she was asking, so he said, "Let's get out of here."

"I'm sure it's solid enough now, Sophie. The other pieces of chocolate are in the box. Let's carefully lift the one with the ruby from the sides with a tissue so we don't leave any marks on it." Jessica felt like she was in the middle of an operating room. She carefully picked it up and set it in the empty paper in the box.

"It's perfect." Sophie sighed. "I'm so relieved."

"It's just like one of the boxes of chocolate that they sell."

"Let's take it back to the chocolate room, get a lid on it, wrap it, and put it on Mrs. Clayton's desk where we found the other box. And get out of here!"

Once there, Sophie pulled wrapping paper off a roll, set it down on a small table, then put the box on top. As she began wrapping it, she said, "Jessica, I'm not sure this will be right if I do it. Are you a good wrapper?"

"I love wrapping presents." Jessica stepped over and wrapped it carefully, making sure every fold had a professional look.

Sophie paced around the room. "Hurry!"

"I'm trying. But I want this to be perfect." When Jessica finished, she thought it looked like the first one. "Is it right?"

Sophie nodded. "It's great. Let's go."

With the package in Jessica's hand, the three of them silently went to the door where Tony opened it and motioned for them to follow him. At Mrs. Clayton's desk, Jessica glanced around as she set the box where they'd found the other one. There weren't any shadows nearby.

They hurried down the hall to the office with the

secret panel. As the panel closed behind them, Sophie picked up the flashlight and said, "We did it! They'll never know."

Jessica hoped that was true, that the bad guys would never figure out that it had been missing.

Tony took the stairs in a hurry. "Now, let's go!"

Downstairs, they dove into the water and swam out of the boathouse. Jessica was relieved to find everything outside the boathouse as it should be. They swam to the shore and got back into their regular clothes. On the walk to town, Jessica and Tony told Sophie about almost being caught.

Sophie groaned. "We have to be careful. I think we're almost ready to wrap up this mystery, and we don't want anyone to figure out what we've been doing. That could make it hazardous."

20

Mystery Man

On their way to class Monday morning, Jessica said, "I'm looking forward to today's class. I hope we're using dark chocolate today. Saturday's milk chocolate and the piece I ate yesterday were okay—"

"The milk chocolate is more than okay. I really like it. If today is a dark chocolate day, I'll have to see if I like Uncle Sal's version."

"You like chocolate chips, right?"

Sophie wavered her hand from side to side. "Chocolate chip cookies are okay. But I'd just as soon have a plain cookie."

Everything in class was pretty normal. Today they shaped pineapple-flavored centers to prepare them for the enrober. Sophie wondered if this recipe was the one that had been stolen. Correction: that Uncle Sal *thought* had been stolen.

The good news for Sophie was that the chocolates were covered with milk chocolate when the students finished shaping them. Toward the end of class, each student was given a couple of the now chocolate-covered pieces, ones that hadn't come out of the enrober in perfect condition.

The candy tasted great— it did have fruit, after all, one of her favorite things to eat—but she could taste something more than pineapple. She finished it off in a second bite but couldn't figure out the secret ingredient.

When they were about to collect Sophie's backpack and Jessica's purse, Uncle Sal walked up to them. "Are you ladies enjoying the class?"

"I love chocolate, so I'm having a great time," Jessica said.

"I've learned that I like milk chocolate. Probably never as much as Jessica likes dark chocolate, but it's made it more fun."

"It's the first time we've had a class here, and I'm so glad Erma suggested doing it. But any tips you have for making it better are welcome."

"We've had fun, haven't we, Jessica?"

"Yes! We'll think about it, Uncle Sal."

Sophie watched as the last of the other students left through the doors. Right when she thought that maybe she and Jessica could catch up with one and follow them, Uncle Sal asked another question.

"Does everyone else seem to be enjoying the class too? I've noticed you speaking to the others. Have they mentioned anything helpful?"

The door snapped to a close, along with their opportunity to follow someone today. Sophie held back a sigh. "I think everyone's having fun. Don't you, Jessica?"

"Every once in a while, Dylan looks a little like he'd rather be somewhere else."

Uncle Sal looked distressed.

"But I think that's because his mom treats him like a little kid sometimes."

Uncle Sal laughed. "You may be right, Jessica."

As he started to turn toward the hall, Sophie pushed aside their rush to leave so she could ask, "Uncle Sal, your pineapple chocolates are super good. But there's something more than pineapple in them, isn't there?"

Smiling, he said, "Yes. A secret ingredient." He paused. "I've heard about the mysteries you've solved and how you've worked with the sheriff, so I think you can keep a secret."

Sophie glanced in Jessica's direction. "*I* can."

He leaned closer. "Watermelon."

"Pineapple-watermelon chocolates?" If she hadn't tasted it first, she wouldn't have believed that would be good.

He gave a nod. "People love the taste of them. But they don't think it sounds good." He shrugged. "So I call them Pineapple Delight and don't tell them."

The girls laughed.

Sophie said, "You're right, Uncle Sal. They're delicious!"

Still smiling, he turned and went down the hall.

When they were alone again, Jessica said, "That's

a strange combination. Someone would have to steal the recipe to make something that tasted the same and that makes this even more of a mystery. We need to hurry."

Jessica reached into her purse and pulled out her phone. "I don't know why I didn't think of it before, Sophie, but today I'm going to take a picture of Mr. P. as he enters his room. It may not be useful, but maybe we'll learn something about the way he's standing or his clothes or . . . something."

Sophie tapped her forehead with the back of her hand. "I should've thought of that. This mystery has been so strange that I've been thrown off. Did a recipe get stolen or not? And why did Mr. P. walk like a young man?"

"Maybe the chocolate made him feel young again." Jessica tucked her phone into her purse.

"Until then, I wondered why he wasn't walking with a cane. In class, I thought he might fall over any minute, but he walked through the lobby"—they looked at each other—"like a younger man."

"Yes. Who is he?"

"Now that we know where he's staying, we don't have to follow him, but we do have to hurry. Have your phone ready for a picture, Jessica."

Sophie and Jessica calmly walked out the front door and up the street.

"It might seem strange to someone if we run now, but when we're away from the building, follow me, Jessica. I know a shortcut to the resort that I doubt

Mr. P. knows about. Let's see if we can beat him there."

They started running, made a turn, cut through the woods for about two minutes, and then down the street through the church's side yard before turning right on a short street with a few houses, and heading up an alley. Jessica was surprised and relieved to see the back of the resort. They both stopped to catch their breath.

Sophie said, "I came with Mom once to deliver a piece of furniture for one of their special, fancy rooms. We used a big elevator near these doors that was for people working here. It wasn't fancy at all."

They stepped through industrial metal doors and entered a hallway that was very plain and clearly not decorated for guests. After going up a back elevator to the fifth floor, they hurried over to the hall with Mr. P.'s room and waited around the corner.

A few minutes after they arrived, he stepped off the elevator and walked down the hall toward his room. Jessica held her phone at the edge of the wall and snapped photos of him. When he paused at his door, they both stepped back quickly. After they heard the sound of the door closing, they peered around the corner again.

"I hope he doesn't spend three hours reading a book or watching TV this afternoon," Jessica said.

"Me too. The good news is that Mom gave us the afternoon off so we can spend as much time here as we need to."

"Yes, but the first person who comes down the hall and turns this corner is going to wonder why two twelve-year-old girls are standing here. They may even call the resort's front desk and ask if we're supposed to be here."

Just like the day before, a man came out Mr. P.'s door about five minutes later. He went to the elevator, got on, and left.

Jessica snapped photos on her phone as he walked away.

"So, his roommate has left. I wonder when he'll leave."

As they waited, Jessica scrolled through the photos on her phone. "Sophie, this is weird. These two men stand the same way and even walk the same way—exactly the same—in these photos. Maybe Mr. P's son is in town with him."

"Let me see."

Jessica handed the phone to Sophie and leaned over her shoulder while she scrolled through the photos again. "Jessica, if the second man had on an old man's wig and makeup, would he look like Mr. P?" Sophie slowly scrolled through the photos one more time.

"Wow! Do you believe that Mr. P. is actually this younger man in a costume?"

"I do. I think we found your spy. He might be involved with the jewels too. The question now is, what do we do about it?"

"The sheriff asked us not to come into the office,

so I guess we print out some of the photos on your dad's printer and leave them at the dead drop."

"Maybe when she sees the photos, she will be able to arrest him."

"I'll miss Mr. P. though. He was fun to have around. It's hard to believe he's a bad guy."

"I would guess that the most successful bad guys are the ones who can fool you. And Mr. P. sure fooled us."

21

Code Word: Spy

Jessica and Sophie wrote their note to the sheriff, sharing their suspicions. Sophie wanted to say that Mr. P. was definitely a younger man, but Jessica told her that they weren't sure, that the younger man could be his son or some other relative. In the end they decided to write:

Mr. Pleckenpoll from our chocolate class might be in disguise.

Mr. Sandoval had gone to a meeting, so they used his printer to print out four photos, two of the old man and two of the young one.

"To make writing the code faster, Sophie, we should make a chart with the alphabet, then put the code letters beside it."

"That sounds good. It will be harder to make mistakes that way."

Jessica wrote down the alphabet on a sheet of

paper. Then she wrote each code letter next to it as Sophie called it out. Their coded message read:

NS QMFDLFOQPMM GSPN PVS DIPDPMBUF DMBTT NJHIU CF JO EJTHVJTF

"I think our message is clear, Sophie. It's up to the sheriff to do something about it."

"It's frustrating that we can't talk to her to find out what's going on."

"She doesn't tell us everything anyway."

"That's true. We often figure it out on our own, don't we?"

They wrapped the note and the photos they'd printed in a plastic zipper bag in case it rained before Sheriff Valeska picked it up. Sophie got out a roll of tape and slid that into her backpack along with the bag which she sandwiched in between the pages of a book—to hide it if this fell into other hands.

When they arrived at the bench in town and sat down, Jessica glanced around, then said in a low voice, "What's your plan here, Sophie? Should I tie my shoes as a distraction while you stick it under there?"

Sophie unzipped the side pocket of her backpack, took out the tape, then reached into the main compartment and brought out the zipper bag.

As she was setting the backpack on the bench, a bee flew by her hand. She dropped the backpack, and it landed on its side, spilling half of what had been inside.

Jessica knelt in front of the bench to help Sophie gather everything. "Sophie, that was a great idea! No one will suspect what you're doing here."

Sophie said, "It *would* have been a great idea if I'd thought of it."

Jessica laughed. "Accident?" She reached for a snack bar that had slid under the bench as Sophie taped the plastic bag underneath. Jessica found a piece of chalk, now broken in two, and kept that clenched in her hand as they sat back on the bench.

"The item is secured," Sophie said.

Jessica had to fight a giggle. Sometimes Sophie got so into their mysteries that she played the part too well. Right now, Sophie was a spy. "I'm going to mark the bench now, if that works with your plan."

"Perfect."

Jessica reached out in what she hoped was a subtle way and slid the chalk across the bench. "Done. Now what?"

"Now, we go to Great Finds. Maybe Mom will let us go to the deli for lunch. Let's hope the sheriff either walks or drives by and notices the chalk mark."

Jessica said, "Sophie, she didn't even want to do this. I just hope she stops to pick it up."

The two of them walked to Great Finds. Once they were there, Mrs. Sandoval asked them to finish a project before eating. An hour later, they were on their way to the deli—with a stop at the dead drop first.

They raced back to Sophie's favorite bench, Jessica barely keeping up with Sophie. She tugged on her cousin's arm. "You're going to attract a lot more attention running down the sidewalk."

Sophie checked around them. "You're right. It's my first dead drop, and I'm excited to see if it's been picked up."

When they rounded the corner and could see the bench in the distance, Jessica thought there was a new chalk mark at the other end. She realized now that that was the one flaw in their plan. They hadn't told the sheriff how to let them know if she'd left something for them.

As they got closer, the mark became more and more noticeable, to them at least. She thought someone else would see it as a smudge. Sophie led the two of them past the bench and then back around in front of it before they sat down.

"Sophie, the chalk mark I made is gone."

"Yes, and there's a new chalk mark on the other end of the bench. I guess that's how Sheriff Valeska let us know that she's been here."

Sophie reached down, pretending to retie her shoelaces, but Jessica saw her hand swish underneath the bench before sitting up with her shoelaces now secure. "I think it's still there, Jessica. I'm going to set my backpack down, unzip it, and reach under here to peel off the bag. Then I'll slip it into my backpack."

As Sophie set her backpack on the ground, the

owner of Buds & Blooms walked by. Instead of smiling at them, she continued on her way without a glance in their direction. Jessica wondered if she'd even noticed that they were there. She was focused on where she was going, and she didn't look very happy about it.

Sophie noticed the same thing. "Jessica, I don't think Kelsey has everything going well in her life right now. She was upset the day she came to the factory to talk to her brother. Maybe he's done something else."

With the florist out of sight, Sophie did as she'd planned. Then she leaned over to see inside her backpack. "Jessica! It's different. What's inside the bag is different."

Jessica said, "Let's get to lunch at the deli and read this. I doubt anyone will pay attention to us, and even if they did, we would only be taking something out of your backpack. And that way, if we find something that belongs with the mystery, we can tell Tony."

Tony wasn't at the deli when they arrived. They chose the table in the back corner, where no one else could see what they were doing, took out the note from the sheriff, and opened it. Using a pen from her purse, Jessica wrote the correct letter over each of the letters in the sheriff's one-line message. Once she had it decoded, it said:

Meet me at the cemetery at four o'clock.

"No! I never wanted to step into that cemetery again!"

Sophie glanced around the room. "Shh, Jessica."

Whispering, Jessica said, "Whoops. Sorry. Sheriff Valeska must know that we finish at your mom's by three thirty. Four at the latest. I wonder why . . . ?"

"Me too. Why the cemetery? Why couldn't she put her message in another note?"

"I guess we'll find out in a couple of hours. We do need to make sure that we're off duty by three thirty today, though, so that we have plenty of time to get there."

The afternoon went well, or as well as an afternoon can go when you spent a lot of it going up and down a ladder and arranging things on shelves in a basement. But at three o'clock, Mrs. Sandoval said, "Sophie, you remember where Mr. Smith lives, don't you?"

At Sophie's nod, she continued, "I have a delivery for him. He bought one candlestick last year and said he wanted a pair, so he would buy the second one if I ever found one. He knows it's coming and has already paid for it. If you and Jessica want to run it by this afternoon, I'll let you off duty early."

Sophie checked her watch and gave Jessica a thumbs-up. "Sounds good to us, Mom."

Once they had gone out the door with the box in Sophie's hands and Jessica carrying Sophie's backpack, Sophie said, "Mr. Smith lives in the direction of the cemetery, so this is working out perfectly."

Jessica said, "Almost too perfectly. Are you sure your mother isn't involved in this?"

"Positive. She would have warned us to be careful, don't you think?"

"You're right. She's always done that before. The good news is, we're going to get to the cemetery a little bit early. Maybe we can choose a good hiding place and watch the sheriff arrive."

They dropped the box off with Mr. Smith, who lived in a small brick cottage with yellow shutters and had a cute little Chihuahua puppy. Then they continued on their way.

"I've been thinking, Jessica: how do we know that message came from Sheriff Valeska?"

"She used the right code. It had to come from her."

"What if someone found the first note, though, and they figured out the code? It's a code that's been around for a long time, so it might not be too hard for real criminals to figure out."

"That seems unlikely to me. They didn't have time."

"Yes, but if that had happened, we would be stepping into a trap."

The two of them walked along silently. When they were within a few minutes of the cemetery, Jessica said, "If you're right, Sophie, and that's a very big if, then we need to be careful. Being careful is a good idea anyway, especially when we're in the middle of a mystery, which we seem to be standing knee-deep in right now. Do you have a plan?"

"I've been considering it as we've walked. I think we should hide behind one of the larger gravestones and wait for the sheriff."

They arrived at the cemetery and walked under the arch that said Pine Hill Cemetery. This moment always gave Jessica chills. She knew no one was in there, at least no one who could talk to them, but it still gave her the creeps.

Sophie put out her hand to stop her. She surveyed the cemetery, slowly turning her head from left to right. Jessica decided to do the same thing, just to be sure.

"I think it's clear." Sophie pointed across the cemetery. "Let's hide over there behind the largest grave marker we can find. The sheriff is probably going to enter the same way we did, so we'll see her coming." Sophie took a step, stopped, and added, "If she is the one who comes."

They settled behind a gravestone in the shape of an angel. Not long after they got there, someone walked into the cemetery. As the person got closer, Jessica could tell it was a man. He came toward them. Then, when she started to wonder if they would be discovered, he turned and walked in the direction of the old mausoleum. When she saw the side of his face, she had to stifle a gasp with her hand. Jessica looked at Sophie, and her cousin had an expression on her face that she suspected mirrored her own. The younger man from Mr. P.'s room now stood by the side of the mausoleum.

He was far enough away that Jessica felt like she could whisper to Sophie. "He's waiting for something or someone. Sheriff Valeska might be in trouble."

"I agree," Sophie whispered back. "Check your phone to see if we have service here. I'd like to be able to call someone if we need help."

Jessica pulled it out of her purse. "No reception."

"I guess that means we're in a dead zone."

"Ooh. Don't say it that way."

"I had to say it. It was too perfect for this place."

Sheriff Valeska walked into the cemetery and did much as Sophie had done: she paused at the entrance and scanned the area before taking further steps. Sophie should be proud that they'd done the same thing her favorite law enforcement officer had done. Jessica glanced over at Mr. P. and saw that he was also watching the sheriff.

"Jessica, we have to warn her. She may be stepping into a trap."

"What can we do?"

Sophie shouted, "Sheriff, watch out!"

The sheriff darted behind a grave marker and crouched. After a few seconds, she shouted back, "Sophie, what's wrong?"

"It's a trap, Sheriff. That man in the photos we gave you is waiting for you."

The sheriff stood.

"What's she doing?" Sophie asked.

"I have no idea."

Movement from the side caught Jessica's attention.

Mr. P. was stepping out into the open. He walked toward the sheriff, but he didn't look menacing, as Jessica had expected. When he shook the sheriff's hand, she and Sophie stood.

"Girls, this man is the reason I asked you to come here. Please meet him."

Sophie said, "Sheriff, we've been in class with him for close to a week. Haven't we?"

She turned to Mr. P. who gave a single nod. "But I'm not who you think I am."

Sophie put her hands on her hips. "If you've been in disguise, why should we believe you? A disguise shows you're hiding the truth."

Sheriff Valeska said, "Because he's an investigator who is in town for a reason."

"The FBI?" Sophie asked

Mr. P. answered, "No, I'm what's known as an insurance investigator. When someone has a large claim—that's the amount of money my company would pay to replace something that was stolen—I'm called in."

The pieces of the puzzle started to fall into place for Sophie. "Were gemstones stolen?"

"Yes. I wasn't certain where they might be. I was working on a tip and a hunch when I came to Pine Hill, but your discovery told me I was definitely in the right place."

"I asked you girls to meet us in a place with few people because we need for this to be in the strictest confidence. I'm going to meet with your parents,

Sophie, so I can tell them what's going on. I've kept you safe until now. And I intend to continue doing that. Do *not* investigate anymore."

The new twist on the mystery had Jessica's head in a spin. "So, Mr. Pleckenpoll—I suspect that that isn't your real name—there are more gemstones, aren't there?"

He smiled but didn't answer.

Sophie asked, "You're the one we thought was eavesdropping on us at Sweet Bites, aren't you?"

Mr. P. shook his head. "That wasn't me. I didn't have any idea that you were anything but two kids in a chocolate-making class."

Sophie and Jessica turned to each other. That meant that someone else in the chocolate factory might know that they were detectives.

The sheriff spoke. "Girls, stay away from the investigation. We don't know who we're dealing with, and both of you know what it's like to be caught up in the middle of danger. Especially you, Sophie. And we also want to make sure you do not mess up Mr. Pleckenpoll's investigation. Let him finish his job."

"Okay, Sheriff."

The sheriff asked that she and Jessica leave before them so no one would see them all together.

As they started to walk away, Sophie turned back and asked, "Are you the one who arrived in the helicopter?"

"Yes. It helps me get to the scene more quickly."

Part of the mystery was solved. Then, without a word, they headed for the arch that would lead them out of the cemetery.

Once they'd left the cemetery, Sophie looked around very carefully one more time. Jessica suspected she was making sure no one was watching them. Then Sophie said to Jessica, "You were a spy, and he's a spy. A spy stole the recipe. How many spies can there be in one chocolate factory?"

"We may never know because we're officially out of this mystery. Tomorrow, we're back to being normal kids taking a chocolate-making class."

While they were in bed reading that night, a knock sounded on the bedroom door.

"Come in."

Mr. Sandoval opened the door. "Mandy Valeska called. You need to have an adult with you at all times until she wraps this up. Understood?"

"Yes, Dad. We understand."

"Another call came right after that one. Erma Clayton at Sweet Bites said a piece of equipment needs to be repaired, so your class will begin tomorrow afternoon at 1:00."

Sophie excitedly asked, "We don't have to get up early?"

He grinned. "I thought that might disappoint you."

Sophie glanced over at Jessica. "We'll survive sleeping late, won't we, Jessica?"

Jessica sighed. "The morning's sounding better all the time."

When he'd closed the door, Sophie said, "Maybe we should try to figure out—"

"No, Sophie. The sheriff said we were off the mystery. We know that someone's overheard us speaking, and it doesn't look like it's the good guys. It's time for her to take over."

"I guess you're right. But it's hard to let go. I'll probably lie here trying to figure it out for the next hour."

"Instead of that, dream about chocolate."

22

Sticky Situation

The morning began better than the day before. With them out of the mystery and able to sleep in, today perfectly suited Jessica. She planned for it to be calm and fun.

Mrs. Sandoval decided to use some of their extra time by having them vacuum the living room, but after that, they went to the beach and stretched out on the sand. Around noon, they ate sandwiches they'd brought, then put their regular clothes back on and went to Sweet Bites.

When everyone had arrived, Uncle Sal took them one by one into the chocolate room, where each person got to choose a piece of chocolate. Jessica picked one of the milk chocolate caramels rather than her usual dark chocolate. She'd been thinking about the mystery—the one they were supposed to stay out of—so much that that's the kind of chocolate she had on her mind.

They used the enrober again in class today,

covering three different flavors of Sweet Bites Chocolates with thick layers of dark chocolate. No jewelry came close to being a sweet treat.

After class, Sophie and Jessica carried the trays of chocolates into the chocolate room. As they used tongs to pick up each piece and set it on the right pile, Jessica noticed that the stack of the candy she'd had that morning was much smaller. She was certain there had been a lot of it when Uncle Sal had selected her piece off the top earlier. Someone must have wanted a whole box of that flavor. Interesting, but probably not important, especially since they weren't working on the mystery anymore. No thinking about clues was allowed.

Sophie was studying the same kind of chocolates. "Jessica, we put white chocolate over one of these. We've been trying to find the exact same piece of chocolate the gemstone was in. Maybe there is no piece of candy like that."

Jessica nodded vigorously. "Yes! What if, just as we did, they insert the stone into one of these caramels, then add white chocolate lines?"

"That's genius." Sophie paused for a minute or two. "This mystery may be coming to an end. If they're concerned that someone is onto them, they may be planning to prepare all of their gemstones for their fence."

"Fence?"

"That's the person who sells stolen things for a thief."

"You have learned a lot from books and movies, Sophie. We better get out of here. People are going to start wondering what's taking so long."

When they stepped out of the room, they found Uncle Sal coming toward them. "Is everything okay? You didn't drop all of the chocolates, did you?"

Sophie answered. "No. Everything's fine." They needed an answer that would throw everyone off in case the criminal was one of the people nearby.

Jessica said, "It smelled so good in there that it was hard to leave."

Everyone around them laughed.

Emily said, "I feel that way every time I step in there. I make myself leave, but if you gave me a cup of hot chocolate and asked me to sit in there and guard the room, I'd be happy to do it." Turning toward Uncle Sal, she said, "I hope you didn't have a large repair bill today for your equipment, Mr. Donadio."

He shook his head. "No. One of my employees opened up the enrober, examined it, and found it was very easy to repair. Two things had come undone and simply had to be reconnected."

"That's good news," Dylan said. "But why did it break in the first place?"

Uncle Sal shook his head again. "That is a mystery."

Jessica and Sophie looked at each other. His mystery probably had something to do with the one they had been investigating.

"No matter. I will see all of you tomorrow for our

last class. I must do some paperwork in my office now." He walked away and down the hall.

As everyone went to gather their things on their way out, the missing chocolates kept coming to Jessica's mind. She tugged on Sophie's arm as she reached for her backpack and whispered, "I should have said something earlier, but I knew we shouldn't talk about this. I might have a clue for the mystery we aren't in anymore."

Sophie raised one eyebrow, then she walked over to the side of the room.

Jessica followed her, wondering if she should ignore her thoughts on the mystery. Making a fast decision to tell Sophie, she added, "A lot of those milk chocolates with caramel are gone from the chocolate room."

Sophie took a fast breath. "Wow. If they're used for the jewels, maybe they're getting ready to—"

One of the employees walked by at that moment, so Sophie stopped talking and pretended to be interested in one of the old photographs on the wall.

When they were alone again, Sophie said, "No one's paying attention to us right now, Jessica. Follow me. If anyone asks where we're going, tell them we're going to the restroom or to stop and visit Uncle Sal. We can do either of those things after that, so it isn't a lie."

It made all the sense in the world. But it also meant that this mystery had gone from "stay away" to what might be a full-blown crisis in two seconds.

Trying to be casual, something that Jessica wasn't always very good at, she walked down the hall with Sophie. No one stopped them. She wasn't even sure that anyone saw them as they walked away, but she did take a deep breath and calmed down when they turned the corner at the end of the hall, and no one else was in sight.

Sophie put her hand on Jessica's arm and whispered, "Don't say anything."

When they arrived at the storeroom, Jessica became even more curious. The door was slightly open, but Uncle Sal had had to unlock it last week. They pushed it open, didn't find anyone inside, so they entered, and Sophie closed the door behind them.

"Sophie, it may not be safe for us to be here. I think someone's working on something here and will be back soon."

"I know. But let's look around. My guess is that the missing chocolates could be somewhere in here. Maybe someone bought them as you said, but I have a feeling about this. I'd hide them if I were the criminal."

They moved several stacks of empty chocolate boxes.

"There wouldn't be a more perfect place to hide a box of chocolates than in a stack of chocolate boxes, would there?" Jessica said.

They lifted box after empty box. All were light as air, so they were clearly empty. When they had gone through most of the storeroom, Sophie said, "I may have made a mistake. The box of chocolates we took wasn't in here. It was on Mrs. Clayton's desk."

The two of them stared at each other.

Jessica felt like someone had poured a bucket of cold water on her. Mrs. Clayton seemed so very nice. "Do you think it could be her? A new box might be on her desk." The door to the storage area opened, and they heard voices outside.

A man's deep voice said, "I thought I'd left this door open."

Panicked, the girls looked for somewhere to hide, but the room was filled with shelves and not much else.

The same voice, louder this time, said, "You!"

As they whirled around, the door closed again. Sophie and Jessica ran over to it. Jessica turned the knob, rattling it, but it was as she'd thought: locked.

"Jessica, I think we're in trouble. We don't even know who that voice belonged to. But whoever he was, he knows we've been snooping in a place we shouldn't be."

"What now, Sophie?"

"I don't see any tools to help us pry the door open. We do need to find a way to protect ourselves when he comes back. He may bring someone else too."

Fear rushed through Jessica. She had to fight to keep breathing normally. "He *will* be back, won't he?"

"I think so. We gave ourselves away by coming in here. I'm sorry, Jessica."

"It's okay, Sophie. I always knew that there was possible danger with a mystery."

"And if our class hadn't been moved to the afternoon because of the equipment breaking down—" Sophie's eyes widened. "That's it! They needed time this morning, when no one was here, to make the special chocolates."

"But why does it matter if those chocolates are exactly that way? If they needed to get out of here in a hurry, why take the time to do that? Why not just put them in any piece of chocolate?"

Sophie was quiet for a few minutes. "It must be because it's a code to the person the chocolates are going to. Maybe they don't even talk to them, but when chocolates come that have the right pattern on them, the person who receives them knows those pieces are important. That must be the code they always use."

"It all makes sense." She just hoped they'd get to tell the sheriff about it. She walked around the room. "We need a way to protect ourselves since we can't find a way out. We know there isn't a hidden passage in here. We have empty boxes. I guess we could throw a bunch of boxes at somebody and hope it catches them off guard. Maybe we could dart around them and out of here."

"I don't know. That might help. But I don't think it would buy us enough time to actually get away. The front door is going to be locked because Uncle Sal will have left by now."

"And he doesn't know we're here."

"No. The only ones who know we're here are the bad guys. Mom and Dad aren't even expecting us at home for a while." Then Sophie stood up straight and tall, shoulders back. "Let's not be defeated. We can figure a way out of this."

Jessica suspected that Sophie was trying to cheer herself up, but there was nothing wrong in that. "Okay, let's go around the room. There are office supplies, paper and pens. I don't think those will help us."

"Agreed. We've ruled out the boxes. There's gift wrap. And then there are the things left here from Uncle Sal's bad ideas for chocolates. There's bubblegum."

Boxes of bubblegum were neatly stacked on the shelves, enough to make many, many pieces of chocolate-covered bubblegum. Jessica still shuddered at the thought, but this gave her an idea. "Sophie, I don't like spiderwebs, but what if we chewed this gum and made a giant web out of it?"

"Oh my goodness! That's brilliant. If we can make this work, when they step into a web of gum, they'll get stuck. Then, if we move really fast, we can get out of here. Start chewing."

Each of the girls reached for a piece of gum. Then Sophie said, "If you can chew two or three at a time, do it. We have to move quickly because we don't know when they'll be back."

Jessica grabbed a second piece and shoved it into

her mouth, chewing slowly on the big wad until it became soft. Around the wad of gum, she said, "This is a little harder to do with braces, but I'm working on it. Sophie, I just realized there's a flaw in my plan."

"What flaw?" Sophie's words could barely be understood around the gum.

"I have to spit this out and handle just-chewed gum."

Sophie sucked in air, then suddenly spit her gum out into her hand. "Please don't make me laugh again with gum stuffed into my mouth." With her fingers, she worked the gooey gum, pulling it into a thin string.

"We need to make sure the door can open so the criminal's whole body comes into the room, not just his feet." She stuck one end of her gum on the shelf at one side of the door and the other end to the shelf at the other, then she stopped. "Jessica, we're going to need something to stand on, so we can get this all the way up to the top shelf. That box of office paper should be sturdy. Can you push it over here by yourself?"

Jessica, still chewing slowly on her giant wad of gum, went over to the box of paper and pushed on the box. It was so heavy that it only moved about a quarter of an inch. She pushed harder the second time, and it went a little bit farther. When she shoved at it with all her might, it moved about a foot. Sophie would probably do better because she was stronger from all the outdoorsy things she did.

Pushing it over and over again, Jessica marched it over to Sophie and in front of the beginning of what she hoped would be their lifesaving web of gum.

Sophie stepped onto the box gingerly at first to test it, then stood on it with both feet and stretched the gum up to the corner she'd been trying to reach. She jumped back to the floor and eyed her work. "It's a beginning, but we're going to have to chew a lot of gum for this to work."

Disgusted by the idea of spit-covered gum, Jessica grimaced as she opened her mouth and dropped hers into her hand. Then she continued the web, stretching it right above Sophie's, but from the other side across and then up, so now the web crossed in the middle. She fastened it, after stepping onto their box step stool, to the opposite corner, making an X of sticky gum at the entrance to the room.

Each of the girls popped more gum into her mouth and started chewing as fast as she could. The web grew and grew until it looked like a big pink spiderweb.

"I hope we're done, Sophie, because I don't think I want to chew another piece of gum, especially bubblegum, for the rest of my life."

"Me neither. I'm ready for some real food now."

"You know, at first I thought that box might help trip someone, but—"

"We want them to get stuck in the gum, and that box might stop them before they do that."

The girls pulled the box back away from the door, something that was harder than pushing it had been.

They soon heard voices in the hall.

Sophie whispered, "Let's both crouch over here on the side where the door opens, so when he gets stuck, we can run out behind him more easily."

They did that. And waited. The voices seemed to be arguing outside their door. Jessica picked up a word here and there. *Snoopers. Dangerous.* None of what she heard sounded good for their future. When she heard the key in the lock, her heart beat faster, faster than she'd realized was even possible. She stayed crouched, hoping to be in a position where she could spring out of the room.

Finally, the voices stopped arguing. She hoped that meant that one of the people had gone away. Maybe they would only have one person to stick to the web.

23

The Escape

When the door opened and someone stepped inside, a man said, "What?" Then, in the half-light from the hallway, Sophie saw arms flailing.

She leapt behind the man, into the hall, and Jessica was right behind her. They raced out the door, down the hall, and around the corner toward Mrs. Clayton's desk. A box of chocolates was sitting on it as Jessica had thought it might be.

Jessica picked it up and ran toward the outside door, pushing on it at a full run, but it didn't open. "Sophie, what do we do?"

Sophie grabbed her arm and pulled her along. "The hidden passage. It's our only way out of here now." They ran down the hall past the storeroom, where they saw a man shouting as he struggled to get up. It wouldn't be long before someone came to help him. When they rounded the next corner, Sophie heard people speaking. She hoped they weren't going to meet anyone on their way to their escape hatch.

The door to the office with the secret panel in it stood open. They rushed inside, closed it, and Sophie hurried over to the wall to unlock the escape hatch.

Jessica opened the box of chocolates she'd tucked under her arm earlier. "This box isn't wrapped yet. Otherwise, it's exactly what we thought, Sophie. These are the caramels with white chocolate lines on top. This box of candy is probably worth a fortune."

The panel flipped in.

"Hurry! Let's get out of here!" Jessica said.

Sophie said, "No. If we take the chocolates with us, we take the evidence, and the sheriff can't arrest anyone."

Jessica stared down at the box of chocolates in her hand. "We almost left with the only evidence that would put these bad guys in prison." She started to set the box down.

"Wipe off your fingerprints, Jessica. They always do that in the movies. That way when the bad guys pick it up, it will only have their fingerprints."

"Check." Jessica wiped off the box of chocolates with her T-shirt. Then she set it on the desk, using the edge of her shirt as a glove. "There's a phone here. Maybe we should call the sheriff and let her know what's going on. This may be the last day these criminals are even in Pine Hill."

Sophie ran across the room to a chair and dragged it over toward the door, tucking the back of the chair under the doorknob. "I saw this done in a movie. It makes it so that the chair braces against the door, the doorknob can't turn very easily, and the door is hard to push open. Now hurry and call the sheriff. And pray that she is in the office."

Jessica dialed the sheriff, and Clare immediately put her call through. After quickly explaining what was going on, Jessica told her to hurry to catch the criminals in the act. She started to hang up, but then brought the phone back to her ear and added, "Ask Tony where the secret passage is."

Seconds after she'd set the phone down, they were on their way out the escape hatch.

As soon as they were both through, Sophie stopped, only a few steps down now. "Push the panel closed behind you, Jessica."

"If we do that, it's going to be pitch-black in here. We didn't bring a flashlight."

"I'm hoping it will buy us a little bit of time when they come into that room and we aren't there."

"They'll figure it out pretty quickly because there was a chair blocking the door and the chocolates are sitting on the desk." At that moment, the doorknob rattled. Then someone pushed on the door. Jessica slammed the panel closed. "I guess if it buys us a few seconds, Sophie, it's worth it. Walk as fast as you can without falling."

The two of them made their way down the stairs step-by-step, finally finding the level area at the bottom. They hurried along, Sophie rubbing her hand along the wall so she knew where she was.

Jessica pointed toward the end of the walkway. "It's brighter around the door than before."

Light clearly outlined the shape of the door, but before it had been impossible to see where it was. "You're right. I wonder why."

Jessica reached up and turned the lock as she had before, and the door swung open.

They found the big doors to the boathouse open wide and letting sunlight into the space.

"Look at the rowboat, Sophie! They must be ready to escape." Several black bags were stowed in the middle of the boat.

Sophie pushed the door closed behind them and heard it click in place. "We need to hurry! Do we swim out of here?" She could hear voices shouting in the passageway.

Jessica bent over to untie her shoes. "If we're planning to get out of here, we'd better do it in a hurry. We only have seconds before they're standing on the dock beside us, and they don't sound happy."

Jessica now stood barefoot. Sophie kicked off her shoes, and both of them peeled off their outer clothes—leaving only their swimsuits on from earlier—and dove into the water.

Sophie swam as fast as she could underwater, something she didn't do as well as swimming on the surface, and hoped Jessica was swimming as fast or faster.

When Sophie came up for air, she saw that there were four people standing on the dock now, three men and Mrs. Clayton, who no longer had a sweet expression on her face but was instead shouting, "Get them now!"

As Sophie prepared to dive back under the water and swim for her life, Jessica bobbed up beside her. The two of them at the same moment dove again.

She followed the stone piers that supported the boathouse and came up for air again at the outside edge of the boathouse. As she did, she heard the sound of a boat coming at them. Jessica came up for air right beside her.

"If they've brought help in a boat, Jessica, we're sunk."

Jessica nodded. Panting, she said, "We're so close to getting away, but I have to breathe for a couple of minutes before I can go underwater again."

When a boat entered the boathouse, Sophie thought they'd lost the battle. Then she saw the best thing that she'd ever seen in her life: Sheriff Valeska standing on the bridge.

The boat landed at the dock, and officers jumped off. They chased the criminals, who were now trying to make their escape back up the passageway. Sophie and Jessica swam back toward the dock, where the sheriff helped them out of the water.

"Are you girls okay?"

"Yes, ma'am," Sophie said. "But we might not have been if you hadn't arrived. What made you decide to come this way instead of going through the main doors into the chocolate factory?"

The sheriff said, "Tony, you can come out now."

Tony stepped out from the boat's cabin.

"I called him as you said to do, Jessica. He insisted on coming along to show us the hidden door in here."

Tony jumped down from the boat onto the dock, where Jessica and Sophie high-fived him.

Sophie said, "Thank you, Tony and Sheriff Valeska. If Jessica hadn't noticed the phone sitting there, I think we might be toast."

The officers led the criminals back toward the boat, all of them handcuffed now including a mean-looking Mrs. Clayton who said, "I planned everything carefully. Salvatore Donadio was supposed to be too busy with that class to notice our activities. Then you kids signed up for it!"

One man came out in handcuffs with the officer barely touching him, only holding on to the handcuffs themselves. Sophie could see why. The prisoner was covered in bubblegum from the top of his head all the way down to his ankles and shoes. She didn't know how they'd ever get it out of his hair, and his clothes would have to be thrown away.

"I thought that the criminal was going to be Kelsey at Buds & Blooms."

"Why did you think that, Sophie?" the sheriff asked.

"She's the only one who is able to sell the Sweet Bites Chocolates here in town—"

"That isn't any reason to suspect someone as a criminal."

Jessica said, "She's been over here talking to her brother, and he didn't seem happy about something."

"I don't see him here though," Sophie said.

"Just in case," the sheriff said, "we'll bring him and his sister in to ask them some questions."

"You know, Sheriff, if she's the only one selling the chocolates, she's also the only one in town who would be receiving the chocolates with the gemstones inside."

"Which is the one piece of this that we don't have. Any of those chocolates."

Sophie and Jessica looked at each other, grinning.

When the sheriff saw that, she asked, "Do we?"

Sophie nodded. "Yes, we do. There's a box of the chocolates on the desk upstairs where this secret passage begins."

"Did you break them open, though, to see if they had the gemstones inside? That will make them questionable evidence."

"No, they have the same design on them though. And we've learned here at the chocolate factory that the design on top says what's inside. The factory doesn't make that kind of chocolate. It's their milk chocolate with caramel inside. The only time we've ever seen the white chocolate lines on top is when we found the first one with the ruby. The whole box upstairs has those lines on them."

The sheriff gave a low whistle. "It sounds like you may have solved this whole mystery, girls. Do you want to hop on board and have us take you out of here by boat, or walk upstairs and go out the doors? Uncle Sal should be here by now. I called him when we were on our way."

"I think I'm ready to be out of the water," Jessica said

"I agree. I've always like to swim, but for a little while I think I'll stay on land." As they walked away, Sophie added, "And away from bubblegum."

They giggled as they went down the hallway and toward their exit from the building.

24

Safe & Surprised

A short time later, Sophie and Jessica sat in the sheriff's office with Uncle Sal and Sheriff Valeska. The girls had run home quickly for dry clothes, then returned as fast as they could. Neither of them wanted to miss a moment of this time when they would learn the whole story.

"Have you found out anything else?" Sophie asked.

The sheriff tapped her fingers on her desk. "We've learned that Mrs. Clayton isn't who she said she was. Her fingerprints told us what we needed to know. She has masterminded crimes in the past, but there was never enough evidence to convict her and send her to prison."

"Does that mean there is enough evidence this time?"

"Just her standing on that dock with those men, obviously trying to get the two of you, would have been enough to bring her in. The box of chocolate with the gemstones though? That was the clincher. Her fingerprint is inside it, and there is a diamond or ruby in each piece. She's going to go to prison for a very long time. She and all of her henchmen."

The sheriff continued. "The surprise was when one of her men said his only job had been to use the rowboat to pick up the package. He claims he wasn't involved in everything else and hopes to get less punishment by telling what he knows. We finally learned about the boats you saw with the spyglass."

Sophie sat on the edge of her seat. "What did you find out, Sheriff?"

"Remember that stolen car?"

She, Jessica, and Uncle Sal nodded.

Uncle Sal asked, "Did they steal it?"

"No. They usually drove in with the gems but got afraid when they saw my roadblock. They thought I might be after them, so they cleverly used boats to get around it. The man was mad at Erma too because he was sure the police had learned something was wrong when she got greedy and stole the recipe."

"What about Kelsey and Kirk Newman?" Jessica asked. "I don't know him, but she seems like a good person. I guess, though, that people can pretend to be nice. We thought Mrs. Clayton was a sweet lady. She reminded us of Mrs. Bowman at Bananas."

Kelsey and her brother walked into the sheriff's office with one of the deputies right behind them.

The deputy said, "We caught them on their way out of town."

With tears streaming down her face, Kelsey said, "I didn't want to be involved in this. Kirk got into trouble, and I didn't know what else to do but to follow Mrs. Clayton's orders."

Kirk put his arm around his sister's shoulders and pulled her against him for a hug. "It's all my fault. I needed money and borrowed from one of the men at the factory. When they told me I would have to pay back twice as much, I didn't know how I could ever do that."

Kelsey said, "I wish you'd told me, Kirk. Maybe we could have worked it out."

He went on to say, "They gave me another way out. They said chocolate goes well with flowers, so a flower shop would be a perfect place for them to use to send chocolates where they needed to go. They told me that my sister would have to help them, or I would have bigger problems. I didn't understand what they were doing at first."

Still crying, Kelsey wiped her face with the back of her hand and looked at the sheriff. "Kirk told me what they wanted. I couldn't let anything happen to him. We're all each other has now. I never knew or even wanted to know what was in the boxes. I simply gave them to whoever asked for them at the shop."

Sheriff Valeska perked up in her chair. "You didn't mail them? Someone came to pick up the boxes in person?"

Kelsey pulled a chair from over by Clare's desk, and sat down, leaning forward with her face in her hands. Her words were hard to hear as she spoke again. "Sometimes it would be weeks in between. I'd think they weren't going to ask me again, but then a box would be delivered one day. Every time, a man wearing a black hat and a red sweater would come within a couple of hours and say, 'I'm here for the chocolate delivery.'"

"Was it always the same man?" The sheriff asked.

"Yes. Always the same man. There's something about him that seemed more than a little scary."

Sophie said, "Sheriff, since there's a whole box of chocolates, maybe that means that the man is going to pick them up very soon."

"I've already considered that, Sophie. Kelsey, I think we'll be able to have the charges against you lessened if you cooperate with us. You shouldn't have helped the criminals, but you were trying to protect your younger brother. Will you go into your shop and wait for the man to arrive?"

Kelsey let out a deep sigh. "I don't have to go to prison?"

The sheriff said, "I can't promise anything, but I can put in a good word for you. I think that you might get off with probation."

Kelsey put her hand on her chest. "Do I have to be alone when that man comes? Like I said, he's a little on the scary side."

"No. I'll have my deputies, Fred and Hank, in the back room. When the man comes in, hand him the box and let him walk out the door, exactly as you would any other time. Don't speak or act differently. Can you do that?"

"Yes, I promise. What about Kirk, though?"

"Kirk is young enough that he may be able to get off with a similar punishment, but that's not for me to decide. He would have to be careful for a long time."

Kirk said, "I will *never* do anything like this again."

When the brother and sister had left the office accompanied by deputies, Sophie said, "I guess we can wait here until we find out what happened, right, Sheriff?"

The sheriff stared at her. "Isn't there anything you'd rather be doing?"

Jessica laughed. "Are you kidding?"

The sheriff's phone rang, and she picked it up. As she listened to the caller, her eyes focused on Jessica. She said into the phone, "I'll send her out."

Smiling widely, she told Jessica, "There's someone you want to see outside, Jessica."

Jessica's brow furrowed. "Me? Here in Pine Hill?" She stood.

The sheriff said, "Yes, step outside the door."

Jessica headed toward the door, and Sophie followed her, curious to see what was going on. When they were outside, a car pulled into an open parking space up the street. A man stepped out of the driver's side and a woman from the other side.

Jessica yelled and started running towards them. She shouted, "Mom! Dad!"

Sophie stood back and watched them.

Jessica was crying. Her mother and dad stood beside her. Her mother kept hugging Jessica close.

Finally, Jessica called to Sophie, "Come here."

Sophie walked over.

"You haven't seen my parents since you were little."

Sophie smiled at her aunt and uncle. "Jessica's missed you, so I know she's happy to see you."

"We had to come to make sure she was safe. There's been a lot happening in Pine Hill."

Jessica made a snorting sound that was not at all her usual, ladylike thing to do. "So many things."

"I was surprised today when I called my sister and she said I'd find you at the sheriff's office. Are you in trouble, Jessica?"

"Not us, Mom. We do have more to tell you now."

"More? Another mystery?" Her mother looked from Jessica to Sophie.

"Yes. There's only one small piece of it left. Hopefully, that will be solved today."

"Have you seen Mom yet?" Sophie asked.

"We just arrived."

"Let's all go to Great Finds."

When Jessica's parents turned toward their car, Jessica laughed. "We can walk there. Everything in Pine Hill is close enough to walk to."

At Great Finds, Mrs. Sandoval hugged her sister and brother-in-law the moment she saw them. Then she stood back and smiled. "We're so glad you're here! Come. Let me show you around."

Mrs. Sandoval showed everyone around her shop.

She even opened the trapdoor in the floor in back to show them the opening to her basement. And she told about how Sophie had discovered it.

Sophie smiled. "That was another mystery."

"It seems we arrived just in time to wrap this one up," Jessica's mother said.

Mrs. Sandoval said, "This one hasn't been dangerous though. Right, Sophie?"

Sophie glanced away.

"Has it, Sophie?" she asked again.

Sophie looked up and at the other side of Great Finds. "Not really, Mom. Maybe not much. Not until today."

The ringing phone saved her from saying more. Mrs. Sandoval gave Sophie a look that said the conversation wasn't over but reached for the phone. "Hello? . . . Yes, Mandy?" She hung up a couple of minutes later. Turning to her sister and brother-in-law, she said, "Our sheriff called to say that Sophie and Jessica have solved another mystery. And she asked if we'd like to learn how it all ended up."

"It only became sticky at the end, right, Sophie?"

Sophie laughed.

Mrs. Sandoval grabbed her purse, saying, "Let's all go." She flipped the sign on the door to "Closed. Be right back." Then everyone filed out of the shop, and she locked the door.

As they walked the short distance to the sheriff's office, a helicopter flew overhead and dropped down to land in the area of the resort. Mr. P., or whatever his name really was, must be leaving now too.

Sophie had one thing she needed to say to wrap up part of the mystery. "When we get home, Mom, we have something to show you about our house."

"Show me?"

"Aunt April, you'll be surprised, but in a good way. And it doesn't involve chocolate."

Mrs. Sandoval shook her head. "Okay, girls. I'm curious."

Inside the sheriff's office, they found Uncle Sal and Kelsey from Buds & Blooms.

After everyone had been introduced and the situation explained to Jessica's parents and Mrs. Sandoval, Sheriff Valeska said, "The man arrived at Buds & Blooms right on time. She handed him the chocolates and he left. We picked him up on the street, so this mystery is over."

Sophie said, "That's great, Sheriff!"

Uncle Sal said, "You two are welcome to come to the next chocolate class. I want to make it up to you since this one didn't go quite as planned."

Sophie grinned. "I don't know about you, Cousin, but I wouldn't mind another chocolate lesson."

Jessica smiled at her parents. "That would be great. But my mom and dad are here now."

Uncle Sal said, "They're welcome too."

Jessica's mother reached over and took her daughter's hand. "Chocolate? I'd love to come."

Sophie leaned back in her chair. "Now I guess we need to wait for the next mystery."

All three parents groaned at the same moment.

Mrs. Sandoval said, "I hope there *isn't* another one."

Jessica looked at Sophie. "I kind of like our mysteries. I'm not too bad at solving them either, right, Sophie?"

"I think we're both good at solving mysteries now, Jessica."

If you haven't read
The Feather Chase, don't
miss the exciting
beginning of
the Crime-Solving
Cousins Mysteries!

One More Mystery

While Sophie, Jessica, and Tony were at the Chocolate Factory, they found one more mystery. Who ate the piece of chocolate when Jessica and Tony were hiding?

To use the same code that Sophie and Jessica used, write the alphabet from a to z on a piece of paper. Then, right next to that, write the code letters. Beside a, write b. Beside b, write c. Make the whole list and end with an a beside z.

Now, find the answer by decoding this:

VODMF TBM BUF JU XIFO IF TUPQQFE CZ
TXFFU CJUFT UP QJDL VQ IJT XBMMFU

Answers at www.shannonlbrown.com

About Shannon

Writing books that are fun and touch your heart

Even though Shannon L. Brown always loved to read, she didn't plan to be a writer. She earned two degrees from the University of Alaska, one in journalism/public communications, but didn't become a journalist.

Years passed. Shannon felt pulled into a writing life, testing her wings with a novel and moving on to articles. Shannon is now an award-winning journalist who has sold hundreds of articles to local, national, and regional publications.

The Feather Chase began the Crime-Solving Cousins Mystery series. Sophie and Jessica dodged bad guys as they solved a mystery about a briefcase filled with feathers.

Shannon enjoys hiking and shopping, and both chocolate and fruit, so she has put parts of her personality in Sophie and Jessica. She lives in Nashville, Tennessee, with her professor husband and adorable calico cat.

CPSIA information can be obtained
at www.ICGtesting.com
Printed in the USA
BVHW030913180920
588935BV00010B/854